Dear Romance Reader,

Welcome to a world of breathtaking passion and never-ending romance.
Welcome to *Precious Gem Romances*.

It is our pleasure to present *Precious Gem Romances*, a wonderful new line of romance books by some of America's best-loved authors. Let these thrilling historical and contemporary romances sweep you away to far-off times and places in stories that will dazzle your senses and melt your heart.

Sparkling with joy, laughter, and love, each *Precious Gem Romance* glows with all the passion and excitement you expect from the very best in romance. Offered at a great affordable price, these books are an irresistible value—and an essential addition to your romance collection. Tender love stories you will want to read again and again, *Precious Gem Romances* are books you will treasure forever.

Look for fabulous new *Precious Gem Romances* each month—available only at Wal★Mart.

Kate Duffy
Editorial Director

THE
MARRYING
KIND

Penny McCusker

Zebra Books
Kensington Publishing Corp.
http://www.zebrabooks.com

ZEBRA BOOKS are published by

Kensington Publishing Corp.
850 Third Avenue
New York, NY 10022

First Printing: January, 2000
10 9 8 7 6 5 4 3 2 1

Printed in the United States of America

To the Muse that put these stories in my head and the editor who's willing to put them in print. My thanks to Kensington Publishing, and especially to Hillary Sares. Keep up the good work!

One

"Look, Jase, there goes another one."

Jason Van Allen looked up in time to watch the third Greyhound bus in as many hours roar by in a stinging cloud of dust and diesel exhaust.

There had been more traffic on the dirt road leading past his farm and into the small town of Current, Wisconsin than they usually saw in a month, and every time a car or bus passed, it left behind a pall of choking, gritty dust that settled in their hair and worked under their clothes to chafe.

Jase's sweat-drenched shirt stuck to his skin, and tiny bits of hay had worked through the cotton, poking him in a hundred places. He was hot, dirty and all but exhausted by the unaccustomed labor, but the workday was far from over.

"Stop watching and start heaving," he said, nudging his hired hand back into motion behind the slow-moving flatbed trailer. "Long as the automatic loader is down, we do this by hand, and the longer you stand there gawking, the longer we'll have to eat dirt and cook under this sun."

He bent and slipped his gloved hands under the twine on the next bale and muscled it onto the half-full trailer, but the waiting hands he'd expected were absent.

"Man, would you look at that," said the man working atop the lurching flatbed.

Jase followed his line of sight and had to admit that the slick little red convertible racing down the dirt road was really something. The well-tuned engine slowed to a purr as it neared. The driver waved one bare arm and called out something that was lost in the wind and the growl of gravel as she stepped on the accelerator and peeled out. The back of the car fishtailed, and for a second Jase thought she was going to lose an argument with the ditch, but she managed to pull out of the slide and sped off down the road, her laughter drifting back to them.

The man on the trailer shaded his eyes. "She's pulling in up at the house," he called out, then had to grab onto a bale of hay as the tractor driver shifted gears and took off toward the farm yard, wringing every ounce of speed he could out of the old John Deere.

The man who'd been working alongside Jase sprinted ahead and jumped onto the flatbed. "Sorry, boss," he called back. "It ain't every day a car like that passes through. And if the woman driving is half as beautiful . . ." He spread his hands, and let the rest of the thought hang.

Not that Jase had any trouble filling in the blanks. He would have bet that any woman driving a red convertible was single, and single women were few and far between in this part of the state. The county consisted mainly of farms and tracts of new growth forest. The towns were small and most of the young men and women left for the city—any city—almost as soon as they graduated high school.

Jase's own sister and two brothers had gone to college and never come back home to stay. He didn't blame them for that; life could be deadly dull out here, especially in the winter when the temperature dipped below freezing and stayed there for weeks on end, and the snow drifts had to be measured in feet. If he hadn't loved the farm so much, he'd have left himself.

But he did love it, even on days like this.

He looked around at the hay still waiting to be collected, then shrugged philosophically. He couldn't do anything without the trailer, he thought, as he started toward the house. And maybe the woman driving the red convertible knew why all the buses were headed into town.

By the time he made it to the yard, though, all he could think of was water. He pumped the handle of the ancient wellhead behind the house and stuck his head under the flow. Then he gulped a mouthful of water and sloshed it around in his mouth before spitting it out. The water was so cold his teeth ached and, as overheated as he was, if he made the mistake of drinking it, he'd not only give himself a splitting headache, he'd probably get sick to boot.

He stripped his shirt off and soaked it, then wrung it out over his chest and back, hissing in a breath as the icy water hit his hot skin. It was worth it to get rid of some of the road grime, though, and Jase sluiced water down his hands and arms, then slicked his dripping hair back with his fingers.

A shadow fell over him, and he turned, expecting to find one of his men wanting a turn at the pump. Instead he found a woman watching him—appreciatively, or so his ego chose to believe. He gave her a long, approving once-over in return. Slender but all female, was his first thought. He let his gaze linger for a moment on the gentle curve of her hips and waist, and the swell of her breasts before he moved on to her face. Sunglasses shielded her eyes, but her mouth was full and tempting, her features even if a bit angular. Jase found himself wanting to trace the clean line of her jaw and touch his finger in the slight cleft in her chin.

She tipped her sunglasses down and he swore he felt the impact as her gaze met his. Her eyes were a startling light blue under dark brows, one winged up in unspoken sarcasm.

He found himself grinning, though he couldn't have said why. Maybe it was the fact that his long, silent perusal seemed to amuse her as much as it amused him. Most women—and men for that matter—would have been self-conscious or offended at being stared at, but this woman held herself with complete confidence. But then, Jase noticed, she was doing her share of staring.

"I've never considered myself a tourist attraction," he said with a mocking bow. "But for you I might make an exception."

"I wouldn't want to put you to any trouble," she replied, and for the second time, Jase flinched. Her voice seemed to caress him, smooth and sultry with a lilt of humor.

Jase took a closer look at her, managing to find flaws. All right, he allowed, it was a stretch to call perfectly manicured hands, well-tailored clothing and expensive jewelry flaws, but it meant that she belonged in the city, and it put everything in perspective. She might be interested in the local scenery, but only on a short-term basis. Which suited him just fine.

"I'm Jason Van Allen. Call me Jase," he said, offering his hand. He even managed not to flinch again when she placed her slim fingers in his. It was more than he could say for her. Their palms had barely met before she jerked her hand from his and stepped back.

"Raelynn Morgan. Call me Rae." She heard the slight tremble in her voice and knew by his grin that he'd heard it, too. She took hold of herself right then and there. If his wide shoulders, muscled chest and arms and lean waist—all of it bare—kept distracting her, she didn't have to show it. It wasn't as easy to ignore the way his eyes focused so intently on hers, as if she were the only woman in the entire world.

She settled that problem by looking at the rest of his face, thankful for the sunglasses that kept her evasion a secret. But when his striking features and devilish smile did funny things to her pulse and dangerous things to her breathing, she glued her gaze to his hair, concentrating almost desperately on how the sun had turned the top layer from medium brown to deep golden. At least that was the excuse she used when she realized he was talking and she had no idea what he was saying.

"So . . ." She floundered for a second, then decided the safest bet was to explain why she was there. "My friend and I—"

"Friend?" Jase asked, just noticing the faint tinkle of female laughter coming from the side of the house next to the driveway.

He started in that direction, and Rae noticed that he shortened his much-longer stride to match hers. It was the sort of thoughtfulness she'd missed since moving to the city, but she tried not to be charmed by it. Jason Van Allen probably didn't even realize he'd done it.

They rounded the corner and he stopped dead in his tracks, staring at the gorgeous blonde leaning against the red convertible as if she were posing for the cover of a car-lover's magazine. Her striped sundress revealed a sizzling amount of leg and left no doubt whatsoever about the other charms it barely covered. She was fanning herself with a floppy straw hat and flirting outrageously with the three men talking to her.

"I didn't realize there were two people in the car."

"Men do that a lot when Chrissy Fremont is around," Rae said dryly. "Overlook everyone else in the room—or the car."

"It wasn't that," Jase explained hastily. "She drove by so fast I didn't see you."

Rae chuckled. "If it bothered me, I wouldn't hang around with her." In fact, she used it to her advantage, though she would never have admitted it aloud. Taking in the singles scene with Chrissy pretty much let Rae control who she met and when because most men simply didn't notice her until she introduced herself.

"Just for the record, Raelynn Morgan, it would take more than a woman like that to make me overlook you."

If it was a come-on, it was a damn good one. Her heart fluttered, her stomach did a slow roll and she found herself blushing like a lovesick teenager. She opened her mouth, intending to make some inane reply, and then she looked up into Jase's intense brown eyes and realized he hadn't handed her a line. He truly meant what he'd said.

Rae had never been one to back down, but the safest course seemed to be retreat. She headed straight for the car, relieved when Chrissy's group of admirers neglected to acknowledge her arrival. And when Jason Van Allen joined them, she made it a point to ignore him. She didn't like the way he looked at her. It made her nervous.

She liked it even less when he looked at Chrissy. And when he laughed at something the beautiful blonde said, Rae felt the unwelcome burn of a totally foreign emotion. It wasn't like her to be jealous, especially when she knew that Chrissy was only being Chrissy; her friend thoroughly enjoyed her power over men and Jase was, well, a man, easily swayed by beauty. So why, Rae wondered, did it bother her so much to see them behaving exactly as she would expect them to behave?

Rae didn't want to answer that, so she turned her back on the question and the people who had caused it. Instead she looked around the farm, impressed by the spartan tidiness of the place. The yard was an open space, perhaps two hundred yards square, with the dirt road they'd come in on making up the east side. A large, white Victorian-style farmhouse sprawled at the south side of the square with a huge red barn opposite it, upwind. "Norge Farm" was painted in large white letters against a red background on the end of the barn facing the road.

The fourth side of the square was made up of small row houses, built to shelter farm workers and their families. Though it appeared that most of the little houses were empty, they had obviously been immaculately maintained, as was everything she saw

Not a shutter or shingle needed mending or painting. Even the wellhead where Jason had cooled off, probably more than a century-old, had worked perfectly. The ripening vegetable garden beside the house had absolutely no weeds, and the grass in the yard was freshly mowed and trimmed, even around the fenceposts.

The sound of a screen door banging shut had Rae twisting around toward the house. A woman crossed the wide back porch. Rae guessed her to be in her fifties, but her figure was still trim and her step energetic, despite the white sprinkled liberally through her blond hair.

"You boys ought to be working," she said, and the men surrounding Chrissy scattered like the three pigs before the big bad wolf. Friendly and pleasant-tempered though she might appear, this woman obviously commanded a great deal of respect.

"Jase, it isn't like you to keep visitors standing around in the hot sun," the woman continued. "I imagine these young ladies could use something cool to drink."

Jase almost managed to stifle a groan. "I'm sure they have somewhere else to be, Mom. We really shouldn't hold them up."

Rae bit back a smile. She didn't know why Jase was so reluctant for them to meet his mother, but she couldn't resist harassing him. "I'd love something cool to drink, Mrs. Van Allen."

"Call me Laura," she said with a smile that reminded Rae of the older woman's son. "Jase, go inside and get the girls some lemonade."

He set off toward the house, waiting until he was behind his mother's back to send Rae a look filled with the promise of retribution. Rae replied with a smug little what-are-you-going-to-do-about-it-when-I'm-gone smile, then turned back in time to hear Laura's question.

"So what brings you girls out to this part of the state?"

"Some man named Van . . . something placed an ad for a wife," Chrissy offered brightly before Rae could stop her. "Does he live here?"

Laura stared at them for a second, then her face creased in a wide smile. Laugh lines framed her mouth and her sparkling brown eyes, attesting to the fact that she did so often. "He did it!" she exclaimed, turning around when she heard her son returning.

Jase handed a glass of lemonade to Chrissy and then to Rae. "What did I do?"

"You mean you're the one who advertised for a wife?" Chrissy exclaimed.

Jase stared at her for a second, then threw his head back and laughed, long and loud. "Advertised? For a . . . wife?" he sputtered. "You've got to be kidding."

Chrissy's face fell and her cheeks burned.

"Of course you wouldn't have to advertise," Rae said, then felt her own face heat. She might as well just come right out and tell him she thought he was the best-looking man she'd seen in her entire life. When Jase puffed his chest out and winked at her, she wished the ground would open and swallow her up.

"Come on, Chrissy, let's go. We should have gone straight to town in the first place." She started around the car, but Jase caught her upper arm, and the lemonade she hadn't realized she was still holding sloshed into her sandal. His fingers burned into her skin, and as soon as she halted, he let her go as if she'd scalded him.

"Now hold on there, Rae. I wasn't laughing at you, believe me." He tried to look contrite, but the corners of his mouth trembled.

"Yes, you were," she accused hotly, trying to shake some of the liquid out of her shoe.

"Come on out back to the well and we'll rinse that lemonade off before it gets sticky." He held out his hand.

Rae flushed at the idea of putting her hand in his, then she realized he only wanted her glass. For a second she refused to give it to him. Seeing lemonade dripping off his nose would have gone a long way toward curing her mortification. He knew she wanted to do it, too; she could tell by the way his eyes twinkled with challenge. She wouldn't give him the satisfaction of pushing her past the limits of her control.

She handed him the glass and set out for the well. Her foot squished noisily with every step, not quite loud enough to drown out his chuckle. It was a deep, infectious sound, and try as she might, Rae couldn't hold onto her temper. "I guess it is kind of ridiculous for us to race up here because some lonely farmer put out an open invitation to every single, marriage-minded woman in the country."

Jase rubbed a hand through his drying hair, leaving it spiked up and looking adorable. "I just can't believe that sorry s.o.b. went through with it," he said, pumping the well handle until water splashed out. "I never thought he'd do it."

"Just who is the s.o.b.?" Rae leaned against the iron wellhead, pulled off her low-heeled sandal and tried not to wince as water darkened the Italian leather.

"Kurt Van Linden." Jase blew out a breath, steadying her with a hand on her elbow while she held her foot under the spray. "He must have gone completely crazy to pull something like this at harvest time. Every lonely woman within five hundred miles will be heading for Current. It'll be worse than a plague of hungry locusts."

God, he must think they were desperate. Rae tore her arm out of his grip and jammed her wet foot back into her wet sandal. There was nothing she could do about the heat rising into her cheeks except tough it out.

"Would you mind telling us where we can find Kurt Van Linden?" she asked. She knew it only fed Jase's misconceptions, but all she wanted at the moment was to get away from him. In less than half an hour he'd put her through some emotions she had no business feeling. Embarrassment and humiliation were bad enough, but the attraction she felt for him was unacceptable. So was the jealousy.

"Kurt's farm is the next one on this road. His house is eight, nine miles farther north. You can't miss it." A teasing sparkle came into his eyes. "I told him it was a foolish idea, but if you're applying for the job, Raelynn Morgan, I might just revise my opinion."

"Save yourself the effort, Mr. Van Allen. I—" She caught herself before she denied that she was there to answer the ad. She'd started her life on a farm, and had no intention of ending up on one. But she had come to document this unique twist on the courtship ritual, and that would be easier to do if she were playing the game—or at least appearing to. "I wouldn't want you to do anything against your better judgment."

His mouth curved in a slow, purely sinful smile. "You could try to change my mind. I know I'd enjoy that, and I'd make sure you did, too."

Rae blushed. Her gaze dueled with his and several smart comebacks popped into her brain, but she bit her tongue. Every time she backed off, he pursued and that was dangerous. In the very short time she had known this man, he had demonstrated a remarkable ability to muddle her brain, and she had to find a way to stop him.

If she was reading Jase Van Allen right, the fastest way to make him run in the other direction was to chase him. She hoped.

"I might take you up on that offer, if I thought you were serious." Rae looked around the yard behind the house, shaded by one ancient oak tree complete with a wooden swing. "It's a shame you aren't. This would be a lovely place to raise children."

Jase studied her for a second, his eyes narrowed, and she realized he couldn't be manipulated that easily. Luckily he didn't know her well enough to see that she was bluffing, let alone call her on it. "Like you pointed out, Rae, I'm not the one who advertised for a wife."

"Well, then," she said and, as if that was that, turned around and headed back to the front yard. But her self-congratulatory smirk faltered when she rounded the corner of the house and Laura Van Allen turned to look at her.

"Your friend and I have been talking," she said when Rae joined them by the car. "There's only one hotel in Current—that's the nearest town. If all those buses and cars are here in response to Kurt's advertisement, there won't be any rooms left, so why don't you stay here?"

"No!" Jase and Rae said at the same time. Their gazes met, bounced away, and Rae gave up all hope of leaving the place with any dignity left. The way her face kept heating, it would be a miracle if she didn't wind up with third degree burns.

"Why not?" Laura asked.

"We couldn't impose," Rae said hastily, plucking the keys out of Chrissy's hand. "Thank you anyway." She barely waited for her friend to get into the car before she backed out into the road.

"The offer is open if you change your mind," Laura called after them. "Dinner is at six."

Jase let out a huge sigh of relief when he saw the red convertible disappear, taking his mother's temptation to matchmake with it. Still, he hadn't enjoyed himself so much with a woman in a long time, and certainly not with his clothes on. For some reason, he found that teasing Rae Morgan and watching her cool composure slip gave him immense pleasure. He only wished he could have gotten her to take those sunglasses off. He'd have loved to see those fabulous eyes widen and burn with blue fire, whether from desire or temper.

"Pretty girls, Jason. Especially that dark-haired one. What was her name?"

"Raelynn Morgan," he said absently, remembering the way she'd smelled, wonderful and mysterious as a summer night.

"Raelynn. What a lovely name. I hope she comes back."

Jason wheeled around and glared at her.

"What?" Laura asked. "It would be nice to have another woman at the dinner table. Maybe we could discuss something besides tractors and crop yields for a change."

"Give it up, Mom."

"Give what up?"

Jase wasn't fooled in the least by his mother's innocent expression. "Matchmaking," he said flatly.

"I was doing nothing of the sort, Jason Van Allen.

All I did was invite two pretty young girls to dinner. One of which you were ogling, I might add."

"I was not ogling her," Jase said defensively before he caught himself.

"Yes, you were, and it's about time."

"Kurt Van Linden started this craziness. Leave me out of it."

"And why is Kurt crazy for wanting a wife?" she demanded, planting her hands on her hips. "You're thirty-two years old, Jason. I'd say it's about time you started thinking crazy like that."

Here we go again, Jase thought. He'd been fool enough to let her goad him into an argument, and she wouldn't let the subject go until she was satisfied that she'd made her point. "And do you want me to advertise like Kurt did?"

"Of course not, but I don't see any reason why you can't take advantage of the sudden population explosion. You're the one who always complains that there aren't any single women around here and you don't have time to get away and meet any."

"The baler is broken," Jase said with as much patience as he could muster. "The milking machine is acting up, and now that Current is crawling with women, the men are going to be spending every spare hour in town. Even when they are here, they're going to be exhausted and probably hung over. I'll be lucky to get a half a day's work out of them. When do you expect me to fit romance into my schedule?"

Laura looked up at him. "I guess you're right, son. I'm sorry for giving you grief when you've got so much on your plate already." She smiled apologetically and headed back into the house.

Shocked, not to mention suspicious, he followed.

"You're not going to badger me any more about how this is the perfect opportunity for me to find a wife?"

His mother shrugged and tied an apron around her waist, then started cleaning apricots for jam. With an expert twist of her knife she cut each one in half, dug out the pit and put them in a large stainless steel pot. "There comes a time when a mother has to let her children live their own lives."

Jase stared at her until he realized his mouth was hanging open. "You're planning something," he said accusingly.

"You're paranoid, son. I'm still basking in the satisfaction of having one of my children settled and happy."

"That was almost six months ago, Mom. You're the original wedding junkie and it's time for your next fix."

She gave him a look that would have frosted the devil's beer glass. "I'm just happy that one of my children has her priorities straight. Of course I should have known it would be my only daughter. Jocelyn always did have more sense than all three of her brothers put together."

"I think I'll call Chase and see if he's done his husbandly duty," Jase muttered. "Maybe if Jo gets pregnant it'll take your mind off whatever you're planning on doing to me."

Laura smiled and patted him on the cheek, leaving a sticky, tangy smear behind. "You do that, dear. I'd love to have a grandchild on the way. But don't forget, I raised four children, kept a garden and a house, and dealt with your father all these years. I learned how to concentrate on more than one thing a long time ago."

Jason sighed. "That's exactly what scares me."

Two

If the little town of Current, Wisconsin had possessed a voice, it would have been shocked speechless. Hundreds of strangers crowded its normally quiet cobblestone sidewalks, spilled out of the doors of sleepy family-owned businesses and ordered so much kringle that the diner ran out for the first time since the cherry shortage of nineteen-ought-seven.

Cars, minivans and sport utility vehicles thronged the four main streets, and buses double parked on every corner, spilling travel-wrinkled women and their matching luggage into the way of pedestrian traffic. Groups of visitors gawked at groups of residents who gawked right back. The two factions brushed by each other but never mixed, like wary rival gangs on a big city street. Men leered at women who sized them up in return, and small children clutched their mothers' hands, staring open-mouthed at everyone.

Rae turned Chrissy's red convertible onto Center Street and groaned. "Jeez, Chrissy. Would you look at this mess?"

"Isn't it great? It's like all the holidays rolled into one. And I get to be the queen of the parade." She popped up onto the back of her seat and began waving to the crowds. Predictably, men hooted and whistled, but one little girl gazed up at Chrissy, so adorably star-struck that Rae had to capture the moment.

Keeping one hand on the wheel and an eye on the

road, she reached into her duffel in the back seat and pulled out her camera. Barely taking the time to focus, she shot pictures of Chrissy, the little girl, then the crowd, though what she saw through the lens sobered her.

Despite its carnival atmosphere, there was an undertone of quiet desperation on the streets of Current. If ever there was a testament to the bizarre turn dating rituals had taken in the late twentieth century, this little farming town was it.

A lonely single man advertised for a wife and his message reached untold thousands of equally lonely people. Women flocked into town, hoping to meet a nice man. Men flocked into town knowing there would be an overabundance of single women.

"Didn't I tell you this would be fun?" Chrissy laughed and slid back down into her seat.

It was touching and sad all at once, Rae thought, to see so many people searching so desperately for love.

"It's so romantic," Chrissy sighed. "It makes me want to grab the first man I see and drag him to the altar."

Rae laughed. "Which is exactly why your father decided he could manage without an assistant for the next two weeks."

"You mean you'd rather be cooped up in that stuffy old studio taking boring pictures instead of having fun with me?"

"Working with Morris Fremont is an incredible opportunity, Chrissy. Your father is a legend in his own time, but I can't learn anything from him unless I'm there." Rae took one look at the pout on her friend's face and grinned. "But I really can use a vacation."

"That's what I told Daddy. He knows I'm having

too much fun to settle down right now. He only sent you with me so you'd take some time off."

Rae figured the truth was probably somewhere between Chrissy's impetuous personality and her own need for a break. But what had really convinced her was the opportunity Current in its present predicament offered. Just as Mr. Fremont had predicted, this little town infected by the romance bug offered some incredible images. It would be the perfect field test, not only for her photographic skills, but her ability to recognize and get good shots.

If she did well, Chrissy's father might even consider her good enough to work on her own. As far as Rae was concerned, there could be no higher endorsement than Morris Fremont's. With it, she could go anywhere, but she didn't want to think that far ahead. Part of the appeal of her chosen profession was that she didn't have to.

"Look, there's a hotel," Chrissy announced. "Let's see if there's a room so we can make ourselves beautiful and find out what kind of night life they have around here."

"If it's anything like where I grew up," Rae said with a rueful twist to her mouth, "the only night life consists of owls, skunks, raccoons and cats on the prowl—and I mean the four-legged variety. The people around here get up early, Chrissy. After nine o'clock you could probably hear a pin drop in the next county."

"Not tonight, Rae. All you have to do is look around you to see there's going to be some serious socializing going on tonight."

Rae swept a gaze over the crowd. "You're probably right. These people look like sleeping is the last thing on their minds."

"Well, sleeping alone anyway."

With an amused shake of her head, Rae inched the car over to the curb in front of a three-story hotel, but when the crowd thinned, she saw a red neon No Vacancy sign in the front window. "Looks like Laura Van Allen was right. No rooms."

Chrissy reached over and turned the car off, pocketing the key ring. "I know the sign says full, but hotels always keep a room or two vacant in case important guests arrive unexpectedly."

"I'm sure movie stars and heads of state pass through here all the time," Rae said sarcastically. "Look at this place, Chrissy. If it has ten rooms I'll be surprised, and there are at least a hundred people wandering around on this block alone."

"Then we'll go inside and have the concierge find us another hotel."

"Concierge? Another hotel? This isn't Paris, Chrissy."

But she was already disappearing through the hotel's front door, and Rae had no choice but to follow. She took a quick glance around at the dim interior, which featured lots of wood and a natural stone fireplace. The deer's head hanging over the mantel was almost as glassy-eyed as the man sitting behind the counter, bathed in the blue glare of a TV.

Not even looking up, he launched into a monotone recital. "This is the only hotel in town and we're full. The next town is twenty miles away and the hotel there is full. Some of the people hereabouts were renting out rooms, but you're too late for that, too."

Not to be ignored, Chrissy tapped on the little round bell until the clerk tore his gaze away from the TV. His eyes shifted from her to Rae and back again, his annoyed frown turning into a leer.

"You're telling me there are no rooms anywhere?" Chrissy asked in a sweet tone that Rae knew masked her irritation.

"Well, now," the clerk drawled, "I happen to have a double bed at my place." He winked and gave them another oily smile. "It could hold three if you're really desperate."

Chrissy stared at the clerk, not bothering to mask her horror and disgust. Rae started towing her toward the door. Over her shoulder she said, "We wouldn't have to be desperate to take you up on that offer, we'd have to be dead."

"So what do we do now?" Chrissy asked once they'd escaped to the sidewalk.

Rae leaned against the car. "We could put the top up and sleep in this thing, but I have a feeling that desk clerk owns a knife."

Chrissy shuddered.

"Our only other option," Rae continued, "is to ask around. Maybe all the spare rooms aren't taken." She smiled absently at a man who stared at her as he passed by. He stopped and started to retrace his steps, but she shook her head and shrugged apologetically, and he went on his way. She breathed a silent sigh of relief. "On second thought, it might not be a good idea to ask strangers for a place to sleep. This whole town is like a Roman orgy. All you have to do is look at someone and they take it for an invitation."

"Speaking of invitations . . ."

Rae took one look at the sparkle in her friend's eyes and straightened slowly in disbelief. "Absolutely not, Chrissy. We are not going back to Norge Farm."

"Why not? Mr. Jason Van Allen looked like a very nice man. A very nice, very attractive man," she added with an arch smile.

So much for Chrissy not wanting to settle down, Rae thought with a silent sigh. Apparently, her young friend had been building a few imaginary castles of her own, with Jase Van Allen in the role of Prince Charming. Norge Farm would be a wonderful place to live and raise kids, but Rae couldn't see Chrissy canning tomatoes and weeding the garden with two or three little ones hanging on to her Armani overalls.

"I grew up on a farm like that," she began, choosing her words very carefully. "It may not show, but a lot of hard work went into making Norge Farm look so postcard perfect. Their day starts before sunup and ends after sundown, with a lot of exhausting labor in between."

Chrissy stared at her a second, then started to laugh. "You don't actually think—I have no interest in Norge Farm or its owner."

"Then why are you so insistent on staying there?" Rae asked, puzzled.

"Because we need a place to sleep." She held up a hand before Rae could object again. "I know you and Jason Van Allen were both against the idea, but I saw the way he looked at you. And you weren't exactly immune to him. You can deny it all you want, but you were working so hard to ignore him, Rae, you practically broke a sweat."

"All the more reason not to stay there," Rae shot back. "I don't want anything to do with Jason Van Allen or Norge Farm."

It was Chrissy's turn to be puzzled. "You grew up on a farm."

"Exactly." She'd never elaborated on her childhood to anyone, and as close as she was to Chrissy, Rae wasn't going to explain it to her either. It still hurt too much to even think about. "And I'm not going to end up on one."

"But I thought you wanted kids and all that. If the man you fall in love with is a farmer, are you just going to turn your back on him?"

Rae shrugged with a nonchalance she didn't come close to feeling. She'd felt trapped growing up, unloved and unwanted, isolated on a country farm where no one could see her misery. As a child she'd dreamt of seeing the world. As an adult she dreamt of seeing it through the clean, cosmetic eye of a camera lens, and she was determined to make that dream a reality.

"Love isn't something you should run from," Chrissy said solemnly. "If it weren't so precious and so hard to find, there wouldn't be so many lonely people walking the streets of this little town."

Her sudden philosophical bent surprised Rae. "Why are you really here, Chrissy?"

"Just to have fun," she said after a hesitation almost too brief to measure. "So let's go get us a place to stay."

"Fine," Rae capitulated. "As long as it's not at Jason Van Allen's farm."

"Well, I don't see any other alternative, and since I have these"—Chrissy brandished the key ring—"I get to decide." She got into the car and started the engine, then looked up at Rae with a smug grin. "You can come with me or stay in town. I hear there's half a double bed going cheap."

Rae grimaced. "When you put it like that, what choice do I have?"

"Absolutely none. Sort of like falling in love."

Three

"Dammit, Jase, where's your mind?"

In a red convertible, Jase thought, disgusted with his own weakness. He'd spoken with Rae Morgan for less than ten minutes and she hadn't been off his mind for more than ten seconds ever since. "Sorry, Dad," he mumbled, snugging his wrench down tight so there would be some resistance when his father bore down on the nut on the other side.

"You'll be sorrier if we don't get this milking machine fixed. There'll be some mighty sore cows around here tonight, and some mighty busy hands."

"Don't look at me," Jase said. "I spent most of the day lifting hay bales. I doubt I've got enough energy left to hold a fork, let alone milk a couple hundred cows."

"The hired hands have all gone off to town, Jase, but we are Norge Farm. We work until the work is done," Emil Van Allen said, needlessly because it was something Jase had heard a thousand times. Something he believed in.

Emil gave the nut one last crank and straightened, gesturing for Jase to back off. He turned the machine on and got a nice, smooth hum. "It's your lucky day, son."

"If this is luck," Jase said, thinking of a broken baler, a broken milking machine and the ceaseless distraction of a heart-stoppingly beautiful brunette, "you can have it."

"Don't complain too much, son. About the time you start thinking you've got it bad, it'll get worse."

His father's words were almost drowned out by the sound of tires crunching over gravel. "When you add in the stunt Kurt pulled, it couldn't get any worse," Jase said on his way to the door. He should have known better than to tempt fate.

A familiar red convertible sat in the driveway between the house and the barn. The passenger door opened and Jase watched about a mile of bare, tanned leg precede Rae Morgan out of the car. Something hot and explosive ricocheted around inside him, livening up every body part it hit.

Whatever the woman did to him ought to be bottled and sold, was all he could think. Living on a farm, where there was no such thing as an eight-hour workday, it would come in handy. Except with his luck, it would probably be addictive.

"I'll let you handle that," Emil said, looking over his son's shoulder and then giving him a wolfish grin. "Just don't take too long. The day's not over by a long shot."

Maybe, Jase thought with a surge of hope, it was his lucky day after all. Since his dad had been off picking up parts for the milking machine, he didn't know his mom had invited two single women to stay at the farm. If he worked fast, Jase figured he might be able to get rid of Rae and her friend before his parents could join ranks against him. By the time his mother found out they'd been turned away, it would be too late for her to do more than get angry.

It wouldn't be a picnic to face his mother's wrath, but at the moment it seemed a hell of a lot easier than dealing with Rae Morgan again. She made him feel out of control, as if he were teetering on the edge of a cliff with the insane urge to just let go and fall headfirst into the unknown.

It didn't make any sense, though, feeling intimidated by a woman he'd barely met, and Jase refused to give in to it. He stiffened his spine and strode over to the car. "You ladies headed back home?"

"And miss all the fun?" Chrissy asked brightly.

Jase raised one eyebrow. "If I'm not mistaken, the fun is in town. But you've just come from town, so you already know that everybody within twenty miles is there."

"Well, that's the problem." Chrissy laughed. "Your mother was right. There are no hotel rooms left in Current, so we came back to take you up on your offer."

Jase flicked a glance at Rae, who was looking everywhere but at him. "I didn't make any offers," he said. Then he noticed she was chewing on her bottom lip and had to stifle a groan. Every time she passed through his life she left him with another memory sure to haunt him.

So why was he trying to get rid of her, he wondered suddenly. Why fight the fate that kept throwing her at him when it was exactly what he wanted?

Rae Morgan appealed to him on so many levels. Physically, certainly, but also intellectually. And she had a wonderful sense of humor—at least she'd been as quick to laugh at herself as she was to poke fun at him. One thing he knew for sure, he got a huge kick out of needling his way under that cool composure of hers.

What would be so bad about spending a couple of weeks in the company of a woman he liked so much? It could be a very enjoyable two weeks and if not, what had he lost?

"Let me have the keys and I'll get your luggage out of the trunk."

So much for making him run in the other direction, Rae thought sourly. "H-hold on a minute." She reached into the car and scooped the keys out of the ignition before Chrissy could hand them over to Jase. His sudden change of heart disturbed her almost as much as his presence. "You don't want us to stay."

"I never said that."

" 'I never made any offers,' is what you said." Rae crossed her arms. "How else are we supposed to interpret that except that you don't want us here?"

Jase grinned. "My mother made the offer, and I would never go back on her word."

Rae tipped her head to one side, considering Jase Van Allen. There was something going on behind those sparkling brown eyes and that cat-that-ate-the-canary smile. She wished she could tell what he was thinking because she certainly wouldn't give him the satisfaction of asking. "Come on, Chrissy, let's find somewhere else to stay. Anywhere else."

"But you heard what the man in town said—"

"We could hardly expect the truth from that hotel clerk. He had a private agenda." Rae shot Jase another assessing glance. "And I have a feeling he's not the only one."

Chrissy huffed out a breath. "Well I don't see any reason why we should drive all the way back to town when Mrs. Van Allen has offered us a perfectly good place to stay."

"Then move over." Rae circled behind the car, staying well away from Jase's position by the front bumper. "I'll drive into town and catch a bus back to Chicago, and then you can come back here to stay."

"By myself?" Chrissy squeaked. She set her jaw mulishly, refusing to slide out of the driver's seat. "I don't see why staying here is such a big deal," she grumbled. "There'll probably be so much going on in town that we won't even be here that much."

"Not even to sleep?"

Rae's gaze shot to Jase's and it suddenly became clear why he'd changed his mind about letting them stay at Norge Farm. There might be ice in his tone but there were flames in his eyes. And she was the fuel for his fire.

Heat scorched through her—anger mostly, but she couldn't ignore the fact that something else inside her had ignited—something on a much deeper, more basic female level. She stepped close enough to him so that her reply would reach only his ears. "I came here to have a good time and you're offering to give it to me. Is that it?"

"You're the one who's answering an ad for a wife," he said, just as quietly. "I'm just offering you an opportunity to . . . hone your skills."

"I don't know you well enough to think the worst of you, Mr. Van Allen. I guess I expected the same courtesy from you."

He caught her arm before she could turn away, and pulled her a step closer. "We both saw the way you were watching me," he whispered, so close his breath feathered through the hair at her temple. "From my side there was no mistaking what was on your mind—despite the sunglasses. Are you going to lie to yourself?"

She actually considered it. Lying to herself would be so much easier than admitting that Jase Van Allen was the reason for the hormonal mutiny going on inside her. But she'd never gotten into the habit of self-delusion and this didn't seem like the best time and place to begin.

"What is it that really worries you about staying here?" he pushed. "Is it me you don't trust or yourself?"

Though it was late afternoon and she was facing the setting sun, Rae took off her glasses. He'd challenged her to do as much, after all, and she had a point to make. "You're overestimating your appeal," she said, her voice as steady as her gaze.

"So you're not attracted to me in the slightest?"

She refused to lie, despite his smug, self-satisfied grin. "There are some things I can't control, but I have every confidence that I'll come to my senses before I do something stupid."

Jase laughed. "Staying here for two weeks should be a breeze for someone as sensible as you."

"Staying here for two weeks would strain the patience of a saint, and—"

"—you're not a saint," he finished.

"I forgot. You already figured that out about me." She opened the driver's door and gave Chrissy a glare that had her scooting over without so much as a peep. Rae slid in behind the wheel, feeling a measure of control for the first time since she'd seen Jase Van Allen again. "Tell your mother that we appreciate her offer, but—"

"You can tell her yourself." Jase tipped his head toward the house.

Rae looked over her shoulder and groaned. Laura Van Allen was halfway across the yard, a welcoming smile on her face and a look of determination in her brown eyes. "I'm sorry you weren't able to find accommodations in town, girls, but I think it will be wonderful having you here."

"Oh, we're not staying," Chrissy piped up.

"Why not?" Laura asked, looking from her to Rae, then to her son. "Did you say something, Jase?"

It was almost worth being in such an uncomfortable spot to see the way the smile slid from his face. Rae looked at him, one brow lifted and an amused, sarcastic grin twisting her mouth.

He returned her look, his eyes narrowed and a slight flush on his high cheekbones. "I said a lot of things. I don't regret any of them."

"Don't pay him any mind, Rae, Chrissy. You just get right out of that car and come into the house."

"But . . ." Rae looked into Laura Van Allen's kindly, expectant face. "We really don't want to impose," she finished weakly, but she knew she'd already lost the battle.

"Don't give it another thought, dear, we have more than enough room. Years ago it took three times the hired help to run this place. Now, with all the automation, tractors, milking machines and the like, well, we have all those row houses just sitting there empty." Laura sent her son a pointed look. "Jase will make sure the one on the end nearest the house is clean and put your luggage inside."

Before Rae could come up with another objection, Laura had her half out of the car.

Chrissy, the little traitor, got out the other side without any urging whatsoever. The smile on Laura's face was so sunny, though, that Rae didn't have the heart to let her down.

It was only for two weeks, after all, she relented with a heavy sigh of defeat. Like Chrissy said, there would be so much going on elsewhere that they wouldn't even be at Norge Farm all that much. And when they were, the senior Van Allens would be

around to run interference between her and Jase—
not that it would be necessary.

Rae figured she'd be too busy photographing the
courting frenzy in Current to have time to worry
about Jase Van Allen. All in all, she didn't really see
why the idea of staying there had ever bothered her—
until she looked over her shoulder and caught Jase
watching her.

Four

If his mother had wanted him out of the way for
a while so she could pump Rae for information, she
should have given him more to do. The row houses
were always kept clean, so by the time Jase had aired
out the end one and carried in the luggage—all eight
pieces of it—he had time to spare. He wasted a few
minutes studying the baggage, a six-piece matched
set, expensive-looking despite its Pepto Bismol hue,
and two battered leather valises, one of which felt
like it was filled with rocks

It didn't take a genius to figure out which luggage
belonged to whom, and the urge to open those two
travel-worn bags was nearly irresistible. He could
learn things about Rae Morgan, things she didn't will-
ingly share with the world.

Things a man had no right knowing about a
woman he'd just met.

Besides, it would be so much more satisfying to
learn about her slowly—and challenging, too, he
imagined. Rae had already shown an intriguing ten-

dency to adapt herself to every situation. She was aggressive when he expected her to play hard to get, and just when he was sure she wanted him as much as he wanted her, she backed off. She claimed to be looking for a husband, but it didn't fit. A woman that self-possessed didn't sell herself for security; she'd settle for nothing less than love. And even then, he suspected she wouldn't fall easily.

Not that he wanted her to, he assured himself. Not with him, anyway. And just to prove his disinterest to himself he turned his back on the house—and Rae. Instead he went to see if his father needed any more help with the milking machine. The barn was empty, though, and despite his efforts to treat the day like every other, his heartbeat picked up when he turned again for the house.

All told, he'd been gone about fifteen minutes, but by the time he walked into the kitchen, it looked like Rae Morgan was a member of the family. Jase stood at the back door, unnoticed, watching her charm his parents as effortlessly as she breathed.

She stood at the large kitchen table, a bibbed apron covering her sleeveless shirt and denim shorts. Her dark head was bent close to his mother's bright one, and the two of them were conferring over a large steaming pot. The scent made Jase's mouth water.

His father sat across the table from the two women, and the three of them were talking and laughing over something Jase had missed. Despite the urge to join the companionable scene, he stayed where he was. It seemed like forever since he'd taken the time to enjoy the way his parents bantered, and Rae seemed to fit right in. If he hadn't seen her, he might have thought his sister, Jo, had come home for an unexpected visit. They sounded similar enough, but Jo's voice had never affected him like Rae's.

It reached his ears just like a normal sound, but within seconds every other sense he possessed went to work. Even through the delicious aromas filling the kitchen, he swore he could smell her distinctive scent. Though they were separated by the width of the room, he could feel the warmth of her hand in his, and the silken slide of her hair against his cheek. Imaginary it might have been, but the sensual onslaught produced a physical response of an unexpected intensity.

Jase felt flushed and hot. His breath grew labored and he found himself shifting from foot to foot in an attempt to relieve the heavy throbbing in his groin. He wanted Rae more than he'd ever wanted anything before in his life and he couldn't have her. At least not yet. He'd have to concentrate on something else, *anything* else until he could get himself under control.

Having his parents in the room helped keep things in perspective. Anyone could see how happy they were, even after thirty-five years of marriage. They were like peanut butter and jelly, total opposites that created something truly unique and wonderful together.

Jase knew his mother and father wanted him settled and happy, but if anything, the example they set made it harder for him to do that. He wanted what they had and that, he had quickly discovered, was asking an awful lot.

Rae Morgan had a keen wit and sense of humor, and she definitely made his blood heat, but if she couldn't challenge his mind and touch his heart . . .

But they'd only just met and Jase wasn't rushing

into anything. Apparently his parents weren't inclined to be so cautious. Jase had never known his mother to share her kitchen with another woman, but she was deferring to Rae as if Julia Child had dropped in for a visit.

"Now, you can't double the batch," Rae was saying. "I'm not sure why, but my grandmother swears it won't taste the same in any other proportions than these."

Laura's smile widened and she rubbed her hands together. "That's perfect! Even if Martha Haggerty finds out what the secret ingredient is, she still won't be able to duplicate the recipe. I'm tempted to tell her, just to watch her go crazy trying to figure it out."

Rae clutched Laura's wrist. "You promised not to tell anyone. If my grandmother finds out I've told you—"

Laura patted her hand. "Don't worry, dear. I'd love to watch Martha squirm; she's taken first prize in jams and jellies at the county fair practically every year for the last decade and then rubbed my nose in it. But I always keep my promises."

"I don't see why *I* can't know," Emil grumbled good-naturedly.

"Because you can't keep a secret," Laura accused with mock severity.

"If you won't tell me, then I'll have to guess." Emil reached across the table and tried to stick a finger into the pot of whatever they'd concocted, and all three of them laughed when Laura threatened him with a wooden spoon.

With a mischievous smile that made Jase's heart trip over itself, Rae dipped her own spoon into the pot and handed it to Emil.

"Don't indulge him, Rae," Laura said with a teasing glance at her husband. "He has a terrible sweet tooth. He'll spoil his supper if you let him."

Emil winked at his wife. "If sweets were all it took to spoil my appetite, darlin', I wouldn't have been able to eat a single meal since the day I met you."

Jase watched Rae's eyes soften and one hand go to her heart before she turned to leave them alone— and spotted him. She stopped dead in her tracks, her cheeks going from alabaster to flame in the space of a heartbeat.

She met his eyes, though, and raised her chin in a dare Jase couldn't resist. He slid a look down her body, lifting a teasing brow at her apron and the wooden spoon in her hand.

Her eyes narrowed in warning, another challenge he wasn't about to let pass. But as he opened his mouth, his mother looked up and saw him.

"Jase, honey, did you clean out that end row house and get the girls' luggage in?"

"Of course," Jase replied. "I'd be happy to show Rae where it is—in case she wants to change." He had the distinct pleasure of seeing her run a hand self-consciously over her borrowed apron before her gaze shot to his and that pretty chin notched up again. She turned to leave, but Laura laid a hand on her arm.

"A woman in an apron is a treat for the eyes and the stomach, son," Emil said in his booming voice. "Long as she's a good cook."

Jase grinned. "My eyes aren't complaining but my stomach is. It feels like I haven't eaten for days."

"Then get the table set, Jase," Laura said. "Rae will help you."

"No!" Rae exclaimed, panicked at the thought of

being left alone with a man who put her off balance so easily. "I mean, I don't know where anything is."

"Jase will show you, dear." Laura patted her arm, then walked around the table and took her husband by the hand. "The food is in the warmer, so it won't take long to set out."

Rae's panic grew with every step the two senior Van Allens took toward the door. "Where are you going?" she blurted out, wanting desperately to have a few minutes alone to get herself together.

"We have to check on . . . things," Laura said over her shoulder, then nudged her husband when he started to chuckle.

"I'll find Chrissy," Rae said, starting after them.

"Chrissy is dozing on the porch swing. The poor girl must be so tired after driving all day. Why don't you let her sleep and we'll collect her on our way back in." Just before they got to the door, Laura stopped and turned back. "I almost forgot to ask you, Rae. Does your grandmother make apple butter?"

"Uh . . . yeah."

She smiled. "Mine always turns out grainy. Would you mind writing down her recipe?"

"I'm not sure I can remember it," Rae said hesitantly.

"I know it's not fair to put you on the spot like this. I'll understand if you think your grandmother would object."

Rae heaved a sigh of surrender. Not only had Laura stripped her of all her excuses, but now she'd found a way to keep her in the kitchen for a little while. With Jase. It was obviously what his mother wanted and Rae figured she'd just have to get through it. "No, I'm sure she wouldn't mind."

"Wonderful. Jase will get you some paper and I'll look at it later. Emil, don't we have something to do upstairs?" The older couple left the kitchen.

Rae took the paper and pencil Jase quickly handed her and watched him go. He was one step ahead of his mother, that was clear. She sat at the table and scribbled what she could remember of her grandmother's recipe for apple butter. She shouldn't have rushed. It was deathly quiet in the kitchen, and without anything else to think about, every sound seemed to tighten her anxiety another notch.

It reminded her of her childhood, of all the nights of silence laced with tension so thick the air had been almost too heavy to draw into her lungs.

She and her mother and father had gathered for the evening meal each night, Rae remembered, her father sour and silent—and that had been on a good night. Her mother had always been so nervous she'd jumped at every little sound, waiting to see if tonight was the night her husband would lose control. Dreading it as Rae had dreaded it.

Ray Morgan had never done his wife and daughter any violence. The only weapons he'd needed had been his coldness and the words he wielded with lethal force, words that left no mortal wound but had been deadly to Lynn Morgan all the same. After all, what thirty-two-year-old woman died of pneumonia almost before it was diagnosed? To this day Rae believed her mother had just given up because death had been more welcome than going home.

Rae blamed herself as much as she blamed her father, though she knew it wasn't logical. Maybe if she hadn't been born, her mother would have been able to escape a man who punished her for something she could never have controlled. Maybe she wouldn't have spent half her life feeling guilty for not being the son her father had craved more than life itself.

Her hands curled into fists and her heartbeat raced, faster and faster until it pounded in her ears and she couldn't breathe fast enough to keep herself from getting dizzy. She shut her eyes and told herself she was somewhere else, anywhere but sitting in a farmhouse kitchen, in the same house with a man who lived a life she'd sworn she had left behind forever.

Just as the room started to spin and grow dark around the edges, something thumped down on the tabletop beside her elbow. Rae gasped in a tremendous breath of air and lunged out of her seat. She set both hands flat on the table and leaned there for a second, catching her breath.

She refused to panic over something that had happened a long time ago. Thinking that didn't seem to change it, though, especially when being alone with Jase only seemed to make her more upset. She had to stay in control, and she would, she told herself sternly. She'd only be at Norge Farm for two weeks. Before long she'd get used to being in a setting that brought to mind the worst part of her life, and she wouldn't make such a fool of herself again.

Right now she only had to get through dinner; that was all.

Almost two hours later she stepped onto the back porch and let the night close around her, quiet and comforting. She loved to be around people, but there were times when she needed to be alone, to center herself. This was definitely one of those times, and the softness of the country night made her feel almost safe.

It was pitch black, as it could only be in the country. She turned her face up to the sky, boasting a sliver of moon and so many stars it looked like someone had sprinkled sugar on black velvet. Rae stepped to the porch rail and took a breath of the fresh, cool air and let the tension of the day ease away.

"It gets warm in the kitchen at this time of night. Especially when Mom's been cooking all day."

The deep, resonant voice made her heart jump into her throat, though Rae realized she might have expected him to be there. He'd not only seemed all too interested, he'd made sure she didn't forget it all through dinner.

"Shouldn't you be doing your chores or something?"

"I am. One of my chores is to make sure the guests feel welcome. Come on," he said, climbing to his feet, a dark shadow against the rectangle of light that was the screened kitchen door. "I'll show you where you're staying."

Rae looked off toward the row houses, one of which had an inviting golden glow coming from the windows. "It's the one on the end, right? Chrissy is already there."

He moved toward her, though she could only tell that from the sound of his steps. And the awareness that rose inside her, as if her body already recognized his. It was a frightening thought and she vowed to keep her head about her this time.

She should have concentrated a bit more on her feet. Chin high, she started down the stairs, only to slip on the third one.

Jase caught her around the waist and pulled her

close against him. He held her there, and for a moment it didn't occur to Rae to struggle. She was too busy enjoying his scent, the way his arm felt around her, hard and different, but comforting. A stray breeze sifted through the hair at her temple. Or maybe it was his breath, and the thought of that made her shiver. Belatedly, she tried to cover it up by pushing him away.

Jase let her go and she set off for the row house, rubbing at the goosebumps on her arms. He fell into step beside her, and although she stumbled once or twice on the rough ground, he didn't touch her again. Even when they stood at her door, he didn't speak, but Rae could feel him watching her.

She caught herself looking everywhere but at him, and her own cowardice irritated her. She'd never let any man put her into such a state and she wasn't letting Jase Van Allen get away with it.

She looked up into his handsome face, but the polite dismissal she'd been about to deliver froze in her throat. Instead she found herself wishing he'd lean down and kiss her good night.

As if he'd read her mind, he did just that, placing the softest, sweetest kiss on her waiting lips. Her heart skipped a beat.

"I'll let you get in out of this chilly night air," he said quietly.

Rae didn't miss the desire in his voice. Or the humor, though that confused her as much as his comment. "It has to be at least seventy degrees out here."

"Then why do you keep shivering?"

"I'm not," she defended automatically.

He reached out and ran a finger down her cheek and try as she might, Rae couldn't help the tremor that raced through her.

"You're right. That wasn't a shiver."

Rae stood there and watched him long after he'd faded into the surrounding darkness, wondering how in the world she was going to resist such a man for the next two weeks.

Or if she should even try to.

Five

The morning mist filled the hollows of the Norge Farm's west pasture. It rose up to wreathe the gentle green hills, softening the landscape in a photogenic way. A white-tailed deer and her fawn grazed at the verge of the forest, long since grown accustomed to the human watching them from barely a quarter mile away.

Rae stood against the fence, her camera resting on the top rail. She'd come out early to photograph the pasture, drawn as much by its beauty as by the peace of the scene. She'd shot two rolls of film, but in the midst of putting in a third she'd lost herself in the tranquility, something that had been missing from her life for the last couple of days. Like Jase.

He'd left her to stew while his parents got ready to go to Wyoming and visit his sister Jo. All she could think about was the brief touch of their lips that first night, and how she'd wanted more.

And she'd been stewing all right, not just about that kiss but about the fact that he seemed to be leading her on—almost making her want him. And when he hadn't come around, she'd found herself getting irritated. Impatient, too, but she'd refused to give him the satisfaction of seeking him out.

A shiver moved down Rae's spine, a shiver she never considered blaming on the chill morning air. It wasn't the slight breeze or the shortening shadows that had the doe lifting her head and her white flag of a tail.

Gravel crunched behind Rae, but she didn't turn around. Instead she lifted her camera and caught the doe as she wheeled and raced away with her fawn, leaving the mist tattered and swirling in their wake. Rae's heart raced as fast as the deer's must be, but not in fear.

She knew it was Jase approaching, though she heard only those footsteps. Like a wild animal herself, she tried to get a whiff of his scent, but smelled nothing except coffee. She even managed to get a grip on her rioting senses—until he reached around from behind her and set a cup on the fencepost to her right.

His chest brushed her back, and Rae could have sworn he paused ever so briefly against her. On second thought, she knew he had. Which didn't stop her from wanting to lean back and treat herself to the feel of his tall, hard body against hers, if only for a second.

"You're up early," he said.

His deep voice flowed around her like the mists in the pasture, weaving a spell of intimacy that she had a hard time resisting.

"It's beautiful," she said rustily, then cleared her throat by taking a sip of the steaming coffee. "Where I grew up it was so flat, almost featureless. You could look for miles and never see anything taller than a barn."

"But that's not why you left, is it?"

She twisted around to look at him over her shoulder, amazed at his perception.

"Chrissy told me you grew up on a farm," Jase explained with a shrug and a smile. "But something told me you didn't leave because you got tired of the scenery."

She turned toward the field again, but not before he'd seen her reaction to his remark in her troubled blue eyes. He didn't like being the one who'd put that unhappiness there.

But he knew how to put the fire back in her. "My parents left this morning."

She slipped to the side, squared her shoulders and turned to face him. "Then I'm sure you'll be too busy to bother with Chrissy and me."

Jase smiled wolfishly, and Rae instantly saw her mistake. She couldn't have told him more plainly that he'd gotten under her skin than by letting him put her on the defensive.

"Besides," she added as nonchalantly as she could, "with all the social events being planned in town, we won't be around here that much anyway." It gave her immense satisfaction when his jaw tightened, but it didn't take him long to fight back.

"I had some of your jam this morning," he said. "You can cook for me any morning."

Heat flooded her cheeks—pleasure at his praise and something darker at the thought of being in Jase's arms when breakfast rolled around. Rae braved a glance at him, stiffened at the amusement on his face. "You must have something to do besides bait me."

He leaned against the top rail of the fence. "Nothing half as fun."

Rae backed up a step, entirely too distracted by the

nearness of his long body. No matter what she did, she couldn't seem to keep her mind off Jase Van Allen, and on her goals where it belonged. "This has to stop," she muttered to herself.

"Why?"

"Because . . ." She floundered for a second, searching for a way to explain the words she hadn't meant for him to hear. "We're not interested in the same things."

His brown eyes met hers, full of sensual promise, and she knew that there was at least one thing they both wanted.

"And what things are you interested in? This?" He reached out and tapped her camera.

Rae caught herself—just before she flinched. Her heart raced even though he hadn't touched her, and she knew she had to put the situation back in perspective now or lose control of the next two weeks entirely. "Ah, at the moment I'm more interested in meeting Kurt Van Linden," she said, knowing he wouldn't like it. But he kept pushing her into a corner. He had to expect her to fight back. "Chrissy and I have been in town every day but we haven't even seen him yet."

Jase only shrugged. "Kurt is really a pretty reserved guy. He's probably hiding at his farm, wondering why he did something as rash as advertise for a wife."

Rae stared at Jase a minute, then gave up. Every time she thought she knew how he was going to react, he surprised her. But she was done letting him put her off balance. "I don't know," she said, relaxing against the fencepost and giving him a tentative smile. "For a reserved guy he can be pretty outgoing. He's hosting a dance tonight. Chrissy and I are going."

"I'll take you over there."

"Thanks, but we're spending the day in town. We'll catch dinner there and go straight to the dance."

"Do you know where it is?" Jase asked tersely.

"I'm sure we can find someone to give us directions."

He propped his hands on his hips and glared at her from narrowed eyes.

That got to him, Rae thought, trying to hide a smile. She knew she hadn't fooled Jase when he straightened and one eyebrow lifted.

"You're enjoying this, aren't you?" he accused.

"Oh, yeah." Rae laughed. She couldn't help herself. "Now I understand why you do it."

"Be careful," Jase growled. "You could get into trouble."

"You didn't seem to be worried about the consequences."

"That's because I knew you wouldn't do this to shut me up."

He moved so fast she could have blinked and missed it—if she hadn't found herself backed up against the fence, prisoned in place by his long legs on either side of hers.

Before she could so much as draw breath, he kissed her. Really kissed her, but it was more like making love because it wasn't just his mouth. It was his body moving against hers in one long, hot caress that stole her breath and set her nerves on fire.

It was his heart pounding under her fingertips where she'd wrapped her hand around his neck, and it was his warmth curling around her, protecting her from the chill when her sweater slipped off her shoulders. His scent filled her nostrils, his taste filled her mouth, and her one regret was that he hadn't filled the emptiness aching low inside her.

The rest of her felt so incredibly full that it only emphasized that emptiness, made it so unbearable that she wanted to beg him to put her out of her misery. And she did, the only way she could.

Rae made a demanding, impatient sound in the back of her throat and threw herself into the kiss with an enthusiasm that should have left scorch marks on Jase's lips. The rest of him sure as hell felt like he'd caught on fire, and he had to break off before he was reduced to a pile of smoking ash at her feet.

He could only stare at her, speechless because he'd forgotten to breathe. Her chest heaved as hard as his and her eyes had gone smoky with passion and something Jase knew she didn't want to face. They'd been inches from taking that kiss all the way, right then and there.

And he had been the one who held on to his control—or so he thought until she touched him. His pulse started racing again, and pressure built, so fast he felt like he'd explode. He reached for Rae, only to have her slip beneath his arm and move out of his reach. She didn't leave altogether, Jase noticed.

"Everyone will be at that dance tonight, Rae. Stay here with me."

"I barely know you," she said, unconvincingly enough to have him taking a step toward her. "No, Jase."

He stopped, took a deep breath and dragged his gaze off her. He couldn't look at the desire still flaming in her bright blue eyes and simply accept her refusal. "Three days or three years, Rae, it won't change the fact that there's something between us."

He bent, grabbed her sweater off the ground. "We owe it to ourselves to figure out what it is."

She took the sweater from his hands, careful not to let her fingers brush his. "I already made plans with Chrissy. I can't stand her up."

She started to turn away, but Jase caught her by the shoulders and spun her back around to face him. "Why do you keep running away? You came here to find a husband—"

Rae knocked his hands from her shoulders. "What are you suggesting?"

Jase met her gaze and held it. "I'm not sure, but at least I'm not afraid to find out."

That made her back off. And turn again for the safety of her row house. Jase didn't stop her this time, but he did call after her.

She ignored him. What could she say to a man who represented everything she wanted out of life, and everything she didn't? Jase Van Allen was handsome, intelligent, maddening in a fun sort of way, and he appealed to her so intensely that she wanted to wrap herself around him and never let go.

It would be so easy to give in to the yearning inside her, which wasn't just sexual, but a deeper need that had been a constant ache deep within her for as long as she could remember. But she knew she'd only wind up hurting them both in the long run. As badly as she wanted a loving home and family of her own, the thought of having those things on a farm—even one as nice as this—left her cold.

And, personal reasons aside, she had no intention of settling down anywhere, not until after she'd pursued her other dreams. Rae had made that decision a long time ago and she'd never questioned it.

Until now. Suddenly her course had become unclear, and she knew she had to get back on track before she got any more confused.

She'd already planned on being gone from Norge Farm as much as possible. And thank God she knew enough about farm life to be able to avoid Jase when she was around.

Rae looked over her shoulder to find him watching her, hands on his hips and his eyes narrowed with determination. He wasn't going to make it easy on her.

Six

Jase had been in the town hall dozens of times in his life. The smoke-blackened beams overhead were the same, the aged knotty pine paneling had covered the walls since it had been milled locally a century and a half ago. Wagon-wheel chandeliers lit the room with a respectable amount of golden light, but something else was in the air, too.

Maybe it was just him, Jase thought, maybe it was only his expectation of how the night would end, but he could almost feel the anticipation in the room. And the hope.

Most of the women there had come looking for husbands, and the men, local or otherwise, were doing their best to take advantage of the sudden explosion in the female population of Current. Including Jase.

He'd already picked out the lucky woman and now all he had to do was convince *her* of her good fortune.

He smiled ruefully at his own egotism. But he had to find her first.

He scanned the room, barely sparing Chrissy and her circle of male admirers a glance. He looked right past Rae the first time, too, then did a doubletake, his eyes practically popping out of their sockets. She looked different somehow—beautiful as always, but in a way that . . . smoldered.

The kiss they'd shared that morning was unforgettable—the feel of her against him, the way she smelled and tasted and the breathy little sound she'd made when she melted against him in the early morning mist. All day he'd fought to get that kiss off his mind. Now all he wanted to do was repeat it.

She'd pinned her hair up on the back of her head. Jase longed to bury his hands in the mass of dark curls and savor her long, slender neck and her full, red lips. Heat rushed through him, intensifying with every beat of his pulse until it settled into a white-hot, throbbing knot in his belly. Her sleeveless silk blouse flowed over her like water, its ice-blue color reflected in her eyes. The combination made him anything but cool.

Neither did her short black skirt. Though it was a lot more demure than what most of the other women wore, Jase still wanted to grab the nearest tablecloth and wrap it around her before she started a brawl between him and one of the men staring at her incredible legs.

Then again, he figured he could fight every other man in the place and it wouldn't solve his problem. Not when Rae was the one keeping them apart.

He watched her search the room, and was well aware that his body had gone rock hard because of Rae Morgan. She looked like a woman with a mission—to seduce. And her eyes were trained on Kurt Van Allen.

She made straight for the other man, parting the crowd like a ship on an unwavering course. The rest of the guys tried to catch her eye, but she only gave them a fleeting smile and moved on, leaving them behind like so many dazed seagulls bobbing in her wake.

Jase had no intention of becoming another one of her discards. Just as he started on an intercept course, though, she turned her head and saw him. Her eyes widened and the neutral smile she'd fixed on her face faded away as color flooded her cheeks.

He couldn't even describe what it felt like to know that he disrupted her as much as she disrupted him. Relief, amusement, satisfaction, certainly. But there was something else there, too, something a bit dark and definitely primitive in knowing she could say she wasn't interested, but she couldn't even convince herself it was true.

He held her eyes across the room, and though dozens of people milled between them, it was just the two of them. In the smoky blue depths he saw that she remembered what had happened between them in the short time they'd known each other, and that she knew there could be so much more.

But the victorious grin he was trying to stifle died. She tore her gaze from his and shoved through the press of bodies until she stood in front of Kurt.

"Jase! Hey, Jase!"

He looked over to see a group of local farmers coming toward him, and by the time he looked back, Kurt had swung Rae into the slow waltz the band was playing.

"You get that hay in yet?" one of his neighbors asked.

Frowning in annoyance, Jase mumbled an answer, but he never took his eyes off Rae. He leaned back against the wall and watched her, muttering every now and then when the conversation flowing around him seemed to require it. All he really did, though, was follow one particular head crowned with dark curls as its owner circled the dance floor in the arms of another man.

Kurt looked down into Rae's upturned face and any fool could see he was already half in love with her. And why not? She gazed back at Kurt with a soft smile on her face, her eyes shining as if he were the only one in the entire world. What man could resist that blend of sensual beauty and absolute attentiveness?

Just moments ago, she'd looked at him like that, Jase remembered, and he had begun to think that it didn't matter what—or who—had brought her to Current. They'd found each other and that was that. Now, seeing her with Kurt, Jase wondered if he hadn't been fooling himself into thinking she felt something for him because he wanted it so badly. Damn, but he was confused. Again.

If she was here to find a husband, why did it have to be Kurt Van Allen?

The song ended and Jase wanted to drag her out of the other man's arms and find out right now, but the next song began and Kurt whirled her around to the beat of a lively two-step. Rae said something and Kurt threw his head back and laughed out loud, and Jase had had enough.

He couldn't bear to watch her dance and flirt with another man and do nothing. He realized he was jealous and he didn't care who else knew about it, or what conclusions they drew. He shoved away from the wall, but a slim hand slammed into his chest.

"I've been waiting for you to dance with me," the beautiful blonde attached to that hand said. "Since you didn't, I guess I'll just have to do the asking."

Jase barely spared Chrissy a glance because Rae looked up just then and her eyes met his, as if she knew exactly where he was. She looked away just as quickly, but nothing could have gone further toward calming him. She'd been watching him, he realized, as closely as he'd been watching her.

So what the hell was she trying to accomplish with Kurt?

"I know you'd rather be dancing with Rae," Chrissy said without a hint of irritation in her voice. She settled one hand on his shoulder and slipped her other hand in his. "But since you're stuck with me, the least you could do is make small talk."

Jase looked down into her lovely face and realized he held the answer to his questions in his arms—literally. He hoped she followed his lead in the conversation better than she did in the dance. She waltzed atrociously, veering off in a new direction every other step so that he either had to follow or drag her around the floor.

He finally lifted her off her feet and put her back down where he wanted her. She sent him an annoyed look, but at least she managed to head in approximately the same direction as he did.

"You're a difficult man to dance with," Chrissy said.

"We might be considered old-fashioned, but around here the men still lead," Jase replied absently.

"I meant your mental rudeness."

"Huh?" A tall, fair-haired man ushered a willowy woman with dark hair out the front door, and Jase's heart sank. He craned his neck, breathing a silent sigh of relief when he saw Kurt and Rae not far away, still dancing. He watched them, forgetting what he was doing and with whom until Chrissy poked him in the chest.

"I thought you old-fashioned types at least pretended to pay attention to the woman you're dancing with."

Jase took one look at her practiced pout and grinned. "Not used to taking a back seat to another woman, are you?"

"No," Chrissy grumbled, sighed, then returned his smile. "But she's still my friend. I certainly can't fight chemistry. There's been a strong attraction between you and Rae from the first, despite what she says."

Chrissy looked over her shoulder, and with a melodramatic roll of her eyes, gave up all pretense of dancing and towed him through the throng of dancers.

It took a moment, but Jase suddenly realized where they were headed—or rather toward whom. "Hey, I can handle my own love life," he growled, planting his feet, and hauling Chrissy to an abrupt stop.

Right in front of Rae.

She stared up at him, frozen like a deer in the headlights. Jase stared back, captured by the awareness in her eyes, the way her lower lip quivered and her breath quickened.

"So handle it, already," Chrissy said with a long-suffering sigh. She grabbed Rae's hand, put it into Jase's and proceeded to dance away with Kurt Van Allen.

Someone bumped Rae, breaking the spell. She looked around, dazed for a second, then seemed to realize they were standing there, unmoving on the dance floor. "Well . . ."

She turned hesitantly toward Jase and suddenly he didn't care that he'd been maneuvered into this situation. All that mattered was having Rae in his arms, the feel of her all warm and soft against him, her hair brushing his cheek and her scent making him dizzy.

He twined his fingers with hers and slipped his other hand around her waist to rest on the small of her back. He'd just taken the first tentative step, easing her closer when the music faded away.

"Well, folks, we're going to take a thirty minute break," the guitar player announced. "And when we come back, polka!"

Rae stiffened and pulled away, searching his face. A slight frown creased her brow, confusion and something that looked like pain tightened her generous mouth.

Her eyes misted over and she spun away in a whisper of silk, slipping through the crowd toward the front door. Jase put his hand to his face and took a deep breath of the scent she'd left behind, mysterious and as fleeting as her presence. He curled his fingers, trying to capture the warmth of her touch, even as he knew it was futile. He couldn't hold Rae captive; she had to stay or go of her own free will.

He sure as hell hoped he could convince her to stay, because suddenly he couldn't imagine his life without her.

Seven

The national and international news agencies had finally gotten wind of what was going on in Current, Wisconsin. At least a dozen news vans were parked in various locations around town, but fortunately, it was too early for the reporters and photographers to be walking the streets. People acted differently when they knew a lens was aimed their way, which made candid shots harder to come by.

Having inside information helped.

Kurt was supposed to come into town this morning, after a week's absence, and Rae had been waiting to capture his grand entrance.

But the morning light had captured her first, the kind of pure, bright sunlight that only seemed to exist in small towns. It gilded the old brick buildings and filled the tree-lined street with intriguing patches of light and shadow that changed second by second as the sun rose. She hadn't been able to resist the clean, quiet beauty of it, and had already shot two rolls of film.

She was just putting in a third when she heard the disturbance she'd been expecting. Rae flipped the back of the camera shut, stepped to the edge of the curb and, barely taking time to focus, panned her lens in the direction of the chorus of feminine laughter and chatter. When she saw a tall, fair-haired man, she took a couple of precious seconds to focus on the back of his head, widened the field so she could get the women surrounding him in the frame, then started shooting.

Almost before the click of the shutter he turned. Instead of Kurt, Jase's face filled the lens. His expression turned from tolerant amusement to one of such uninhibited joy the sunrise paled in comparison. Rae tightened her index finger, kept it clenched long after the whir of the automatic shutter stopped, regretting that she only had thirty-six exposures to spend on one of the most incredible faces she'd ever seen.

And then he was walking toward her with a loose, unhurried stride, his long legs devouring the distance between them. Though that heart-stopping smile was still on his handsome face, the spell was broken. Rae couldn't continue to watch, not if she wanted to draw breath anytime soon. She dropped her eyes, backed up on weak legs until she felt the comforting bulk of the brick wall at her back, and fumbled to replace the roll of film she'd just wasted. . . .

No, she couldn't quite bring herself to call it a waste. There was no way to put a price on how it felt to know that seeing her had put a smile like that on Jase's face. It felt incredible and confusing and more than a little scary.

"You could have a lot more of me than a picture."

Although she knew Jase was there, the sound of his deep voice made her start, so violently that she exposed half the roll of film she was trying to load in her camera.

She kept her eyes on her fumbling hands. "At the moment I just want you to go away."

"I'd believe that if you hadn't just taken enough pictures of me to paper a wall."

"I thought you were Kurt," she mumbled, almost wishing he was.

After his tenderness at the dance, she still felt too vulnerable to face him. She'd endured a long, sleepless night, but having her camera in her hand went a long way toward restoring her equilibrium.

With one smile, Jase had ruined all her hard work.

"But I'm much more handsome, don't you think?"

Rae didn't need to see his grin, she could hear it in his voice, and her own lips twitched in response. "With an ego like that, you don't need my opinion." She lifted her eyes to his and though she thought she'd prepared herself, his gaze shocked through her like a jolt of raw electricity.

"I'd like to hear it anyway," he said, his voice low and intimate. "Have lunch with me."

Rae opened her mouth, but she had to force some air back into her lungs before she could speak. She hated the weakness, hated being so susceptible to Jase that she couldn't manage to breathe, let alone keep her priorities straight. "I'm having lunch with Kurt," she finally managed.

"Oh. Are you planning to ambush him with that?" he asked, gesturing to the camera hanging around her neck.

Rae cradled her favorite Nikon in a protective hand. "Kurt agreed to be photographed. I'm just waiting for him to pick me up."

Jase managed to keep the smile on his face, but he knew jealousy had roared to life in his eyes. Perhaps her relationship with his neighbor was strictly business, but he wasn't sure. "Well, Kurt and I are old friends. He won't mind if I join you."

"But I will." Rae swung around and walked away. Jase started after her, but before he'd gone two steps he thought better of it. He'd been chasing Rae for a week now, harder and faster every time she resisted. And she resisted a hell of a lot for a woman who'd kissed him as if he were the answer to the meaning of life.

It was time to take a step back, he thought, time to regroup and decide what he wanted from Rae Morgan. And when he'd examined his heart and made up his mind, nothing she could do was going to change either.

The lovely sunrise had ripened into a day as perfect as a picture postcard. Rae's hair tickled against her bare shoulders and the branches of the huge old oak at her back whispered with a light, balmy breeze. The air was rich with the scents of grass and wildflowers crushed beneath the plaid wool stadium blanket Kurt had spread on the highest hill on his farm. Birds sang, bees buzzed, and the sun shone like a benediction.

Rae sat on a corner of the blanket, absent-mindedly tearing the petals off a daisy. Her mind drifted lazily, but she half-listened to her host. It would be rude not to—considering the fact that Chrissy had wandered off toward the duck pond over an hour ago.

"Really, Kurt," she said, stifling a yawn. "You don't have to apologize. It's been so hectic the last week. I can't think of anything more restful than a picnic." Actually, she'd have liked to stretch out and take a nap, but that had nothing to do with the social whirl. She refused to think about what—or rather who— was behind her lack of sleep.

"Unfortunately, I've become a celebrity. If we tried to eat at the diner in town, there'd be no peace."

Rae shuddered. "And we'd probably wind up on the evening news."

"Yeah," Kurt agreed glumly. "That's why I thought a picnic would be better. I almost wish I'd never placed that ad, except . . ." His eyes wandered to Chrissy, standing over by the pond, her hair shining gold-bright in the sun and her dress billowing gently around her slender body. "I'd appreciate it if you put in a good word for me," he said softly.

"I'll try, Kurt, but Chrissy is . . . Chrissy," Rae finished for lack of anything better.

Kurt sighed heavily. "I know what you mean. She defies description, but that's what draws me to her. My life has always been so . . . not boring, exactly. Maybe routine is the word I'm looking for. Hell, you could set a clock by me, Rae. I do the same thing at the same time every day, until the days just seem to run together. Thank God I live in a place that has four seasons or I probably wouldn't even notice the passage of time."

"I know exactly what you mean, Kurt." Rae plucked another flower and twirled it between her thumb and forefinger before she went to work stripping it down to a bare stem. "I grew up on a farm."

"Don't get me wrong," Kurt said hastily. "I wouldn't be here unless I wanted to."

"I moved to Chicago when I was eighteen and I never looked back."

He glanced over at Rae, seeing his own unhappiness mirrored on her face. "Until now?"

Her head jerked up and she flushed hotly at the understanding in his eyes.

"It seems Jase and I have the same problem," Kurt added.

"Jase's problem is that he won't take no for an answer," Rae muttered crossly. Except she didn't know who she was mad at, Jase or herself.

"Speak of the devil."

Kurt pointed over her shoulder, and Rae twisted around, groaning when she saw Jase striding across the pasture toward their hill.

He took off his baseball cap and waved when he saw her watching. The sun glinted in his hair, and his jeans and white T-shirt molded to the hard planes of his body, moving with the flex of his thighs and the swing of his arms. He looked so strong and vital that Rae's heart leaped into her throat, fluttering like a caged bird. She reached for her camera, desperate to capture him on film like that, with the lush farmland spread out behind him. He belonged here, she thought, and she didn't.

But she wanted to.

That realization slammed into her just as her hand came up empty. She'd shot pictures of Kurt's farm, then left her camera in Chrissy's car. She had half-expected Jase to show up, and it hadn't seemed like a good idea to have it along.

Jase was just too observant, already too close to figuring out why she carried a camera so often. And if she had a hard time keeping that a secret, how on earth, she wondered, was she going to hide the fact that she was halfway to falling in love with him?

Panic raced through her and she surged to her feet, planning to run, anywhere as long as it wasn't toward Jase. But Kurt caught her by the hand and stopped her.

"It won't do you any good, Rae."

She met his eyes, knew that he understood. "I just need some time to think." She squeezed his hand and managed a smile. "And while I'm at it, I'll nag Chrissy into spending some time with you."

"Don't, Rae. If she has to be forced . . ." He shrugged, his gaze wandering to where Chrissy stood throwing bread to the ducks and geese crowded at her feet.

He looked so miserable it broke her heart. Chrissy might be her best friend, but just then Rae wanted to drag her back and make her give Kurt a chance. And then she realized she wasn't exactly giving Jase the benefit of the doubt.

"Chrissy can't be pushed into anything she doesn't want to do. She has a will of iron." Unlike me, Rae thought derisively. She couldn't seem to keep her own path firmly in sight when Jase planted himself in the middle of it. Now he even had her feeling guilty for trying to shove him aside, even though it was his own fault for trying to bull his way into her life.

"I've noticed." Kurt got to his feet. "You'd better take off if you want some time alone." He jerked a thumb over his shoulder. "I'll stall him."

Rae lifted up to her toes and kissed his cheek. "Thanks, Kurt. I owe you one." She turned and hurried down the hill.

Kurt turned around in time to see Jase plant his feet in the middle of the blanket. His fists were clenched and he had the light of battle in his eyes.

"Pitchforks at dawn?"

"Don't be an idiot," Jase growled, shouldering past him.

Kurt grabbed his arm and swung him back around. "Why don't you let her alone for a few minutes, Jase."

"Are you interested in her?"

"I think she could be a friend," Kurt said, looking after her. "Maybe the sister I never had."

"That was no sisterly kiss I saw."

"That's because you saw it through a haze of green."

Jase snorted. "Am I imagining that she keeps running away from me, too?"

"No more than I'm imagining that Chrissy stays as far away from me as she can."

Jase closed his eyes and shook his head, all his anger draining away. He was bone-weary of chasing Rae, but he wanted her so much he ached with it. "So what do we do now?"

"If I knew that I wouldn't be on top of this hill with your ugly face for company."

"You're not exactly what I had in mind, either," Jase said dryly.

They both looked toward the duck pond, to the bright head and the dark one bent together in conversation. As they watched, Chrissy turned and headed toward them.

"Looks like your luck just changed," Jase said. "I guess I'll just have to make my own."

Rae dropped down onto the rocky ground, wrapped her arms around her legs and rested her chin on her knees. It had been so easy to tell Chrissy what to do. It wasn't so simple when her own heart was at risk.

But she wasn't the only one involved, Rae acknowledged, and she had to start taking that into consideration. Jase threatened everything she wanted out of life, but malice didn't guide his actions.

She didn't want to think about what might be motivating him. Yet she couldn't help but remember the hurt that had flashed across his eyes at the dance when she'd walked away from him. And she couldn't deny the heat that flashed between them whenever he got too close.

So what did it all mean? she wondered. What was she so afraid of? If she let Jase into her life—

Rae heard footsteps behind her and sighed. She should have known he wouldn't leave her alone for long.

"You must be thinking about me," he said, dropping down beside her and tapping the back of one of her hands.

Rae realized she'd clenched her fists in frustration, and no wonder. She'd been on the verge of making a decision she had agonized over for what felt like forever. And now he'd crowd her again, and she'd be right back to acting on impulse, prompted by feelings she didn't understand and fears she couldn't control.

As if he'd read her mind, he scooted closer to her, so that barely an inch of air separated his hip from hers and he had to lean back so his wide shoulders didn't bump hers.

She felt surrounded, closed in, and though she knew it was childish, she moved a foot away. He followed. Rae blew out a breath of air that lifted the bangs off her forehead and shifted to the side again.

Again Jase slid next to her.

She dropped her forehead to her knees, managing to shut out his disturbing presence long enough to take stock of the situation—and the first thing she noticed was that her backside hurt.

Rae moved over again, putting out a hand to stop

Jase from following her. She plucked a stone out of the grass where she'd been sitting. It had felt like a boulder a moment ago, but it was barely bigger than her knuckle. It was funny, she thought, how the things that hurt always seemed bigger than they were until you got a good, close look at them.

She tossed the rock into the water, wishing she could do the same with her troubles, but Jase was too big to pick up, let alone throw. Rae shot a longing glance over her shoulder, wishing she could escape back to Kurt and Chrissy's company where she'd be safe. It wouldn't solve anything, though, and she'd grown tired of hiding from Jase and everything he made her feel.

"Worried that your friend is moving in on your territory?" Jase heard the harshness in his voice and tried to temper it with reason. He didn't understand the speed and depth of his feelings for Rae. How could he expect her to accept, let alone return those feelings? But it stung to see her pull away from him, and he needed to know why she kept doing it.

"I know Kurt isn't interested in you, and I don't think you're interested in him, Rae. So what's really going on?"

"I . . . I'm just having lunch with friends."

"Kurt's half in love with Chrissy. I'd hate to think you're using him to—"

"I don't use people," Rae shot back. But she did, she admitted to herself. She had been using Kurt a little, just to put Jase off. Thinking of it like that smarted.

She blushed, and suddenly all her reasons for keeping her dream a secret weren't good enough. She wanted to tell him the truth—but the truth was, she just wasn't ready.

Jase had already gotten past so many of her defenses. If he knew how important photography was to her, he'd finagle his way around that, too. She didn't think he'd try to change her mind about having a career. What worried her was that he'd accept it, become a willing participant even.

Photography had been her salvation, though she knew some would say it had become a crutch. It kept her facing forward, and gave her a safe distance from which to look at the world. If she didn't like what she saw through the lens, she could put on a filter, or focus somewhere else entirely. Whenever the darkness of her childhood threatened to crawl back into her life, she turned to her camera. It made her feel like she was in control, because everything turned out pretty much the way she wanted in her pictures.

Photography had given her comfort, self-confidence, and the courage to have a dream and go after it. She didn't want to lose that. She couldn't afford to.

"Fine," Jase said, dragging her back to Kurt's duck pond and one of those difficult situations she'd always managed to avoid.

"You're not ready to trust me yet, Rae. I can wait." And he would, Jase thought, though he hated the necessity of it. It felt like he'd wanted her forever, and that he would want her for the rest of his life, but he had to go slow or he might push her away for good.

He couldn't afford to do that before he found out why she kept running. She might not want anything to do with him, he thought bleakly. But he honestly didn't think he'd mistaken the way she reacted to him. Or that Rae was the type of woman who would react to him so strongly on a physical level without something deeper behind it.

"The county fair starts tomorrow," he said on a flash of inspiration. "Go with me."

"I don't know . . ."

"I'm taking Mom's jam over there to enter it for her, but it's really your recipe. You should be there, too."

"It's my grandmother's recipe," Rae pointed out, but she heard the weakness in her own voice and knew Jase hadn't missed it either.

"Rae, I won't take no for an answer."

"All right," she said, smiling when she saw the surprise on his face. She really didn't have the heart to turn him down again, and in her heart she really didn't want to. Besides, she reasoned, if she was going to be safe with Jase anywhere, the county fair ought to be it.

Eight

Rae had forgotten how fun a fair could be. From the moment the top of the ferris wheel came into view and the rest of the tents, rides and buildings unfolded beneath, she'd felt ten years old again. She wanted to run across the already trampled grass and gorge herself on everything she smelled—cotton candy and caramel apples, popcorn and spicy sausage.

Instead of hurting her ears, the loud stutter of the motors running the rides made her insides tremble in anticipation, and the screams of the riders sent a thrill of excitement dancing over her skin.

She turned around to thank Jase for bringing her, but he was gone, so she stopped next to the fence surrounding the Tilt-A-Whirl to wait for him.

A girl and a boy about ten and twelve years old raced up next to her and stared wistfully at the speeding cars whipping around in ever faster circles. Rae knew just how they felt. She remembered spinning around so fast the world became a dizzying blur, laughing 'til tears rolled down her face, then begging her grandmother to let her ride again and again.

After her mother died, the yearly county fair had been the one remotely social event her father had attended, and only because it would benefit the farm if he won the livestock event.

She caught sight of Jase coming toward her and reburied the unpleasant memories as deeply in her mind as she could.

She didn't even try to stop the smile of welcome that curved her lips. It felt too good, being here with him, and if he knew she was enjoying herself, so what? But instead of joining her, he veered off. She watched, puzzled as Jase crouched down by the watching kids, handing them something that made their faces light up. The boy grabbed the little girl's hand and, laughing, they ran around to where the line snaked toward the entrance.

Rae's heart lurched with something she didn't want to recognize as tenderness. But there was no getting around the fact that it was impossible to resist such a generous, sweet gesture. "That was a wonderful thing to do," she said when Jase joined her at the fence.

"What if I tell you those were our ride tickets?"

Rae sucked in a breath. She tried to tell herself she'd just dodged a bullet, but all she could think of was how it would have felt to be crushed up against Jase, the whole long, hard length of him, by centrifugal force. Her head buzzed and she tried to take a deep breath before she fainted. "Guess I'll have to forgive you," she teased weakly.

"So what do you want to do instead?" he asked, grinning down at her.

Ride the Tilt-A-Whirl, Rae thought, struggling to get hold of her runaway emotions.

"There're the livestock exhibits," Jase continued, "the horse show, the tractor races, and I think there's a butter churning competition later this afternoon."

Rae laughed, a bit shaky at first, then stronger as she managed to block her imagination. "You forgot about the jam."

"The judging isn't until seven o'clock tonight."

"Another one of those little details you forgot to mention when you invited me to the fair?" she asked, arching a brow. "Like the fact that it took us two hours to get here."

Jase grinned. "And it will take us two hours to get back home."

"After the judging."

"That won't last all that long." He took her elbow, and steered her away from the screams and loud music near the rides.

Rae held her breath as warmth spread, and when his fingers slipped away in an all-too-brief caress, she didn't know whether to be relieved or disappointed. "Don't forget I grew up on a farm," she said, trying to hide the way a simple touch of his hand affected her. "I've been to these things before, Jase. A judging can take hours."

"True."

"I can sleep in tomorrow," she pointed out, "but you have to get up early. You'll be exhausted."

"Your pleasure is worth a few hours of lost sleep," he said, glancing down at her.

His gaze barely met hers before moving away, but Rae didn't think she'd imagined the way his eyes had burned into hers for that fraction of a second, as if he meant a different sort of pleasure than a sunny day at the county fair. Or maybe she was the one who couldn't keep her mind out of the bedroom.

There was no denying the fact that his mention of pleasure made her think of his lips of hers, his hands caressing her bare skin. She could almost feel the heat of his work-roughened fingertips brushing across her breasts. A shudder raced through her and goosebumps moved over her arms in waves, banished by the hot sun almost as fast as they rose.

Rae peeked up at Jase, hoping he hadn't noticed her upheaval. For a second she thought she saw his lips twitching, but when he looked down at her again, his smile was benign and his eyes sparkled with nothing more than his normal good humor.

She didn't buy it for a minute, but she had to give him high marks for his performance. Definitely Hollywood caliber, she thought dryly. But she couldn't be absolutely sure he was playing games, and in any case, she'd decided to open her mind, if not her heart, and give him the benefit of the doubt.

"You hungry?"

Rae sent Jase a sideways glance, both brows raised in disbelief. She'd been trying not to breathe, let alone think about food while they toured the live-stock enclosures.

The cow barns hadn't been too bad. Neither were the horses, pigs and sheep; they were all kept in large, well-ventilated buildings with ready water supplies so the animals could be bathed and groomed before they were judged. The chickens and rabbits, however, were kept in a smaller building, the few open windows not enough to dispel the odor of dozens of caged animals.

Rae paused in the doorway of yet another airless room, trying to calm her swimming head and rolling stomach. "I can't believe you're talking about food." But she knew it wasn't just the smell making her nauseous and claustrophobic. It was the memories.

Jase must have seen the tinge of green on her face because he set his palm between her shoulder blades and propelled her out into the sunshine.

"You should have told me it was getting to you," he scolded, his voice harsh. "We could have done something else."

"You said you needed some new roosters."

"Not badly enough to have you get sick for it."

"I'm not sick," Rae protested. But she leaned back against the brick wall of the building, soaking up fresh air and freedom until her stomach and her head stopped spinning.

Jase pulled his cap off and ran his hand back through his hair, looking everywhere but at her. He seemed so genuinely upset that Rae felt instant remorse.

"I'm sorry, Jase. I guess I didn't realize it was bothering me until it was almost too late."

His jaw tensed once, then relaxed as he looked

down at her. "It's probably because you haven't eaten all day."

She sucked in a deep breath, grateful when her stomach didn't roll. "Then feed me—as long as it's not something that moos, clucks or oinks."

A slow, wide smile blossomed on Jase's face and warmed Rae all the way to her bones. She pushed away from the wall, falling into step beside him because it was better than launching herself into his arms the way she wanted to.

Her desire shocked her, not only the strength of it, but the fact that it was getting harder to fight.

Jase left her at a small table under a red and white striped awning, open on all four sides. Rae hardly noticed the canvas snapping in the warm summer breeze, the mouth-watering aromas, or the children running and playing between the tables. She sank down on the hard metal chair, weary to the depths of her soul, but not from lack of sleep.

She was tired of being at war, with herself and Jase, tired of seeing unhappiness on his handsome face and knowing she'd put it there. Tired of her own confusion.

She could have blamed Jase, but it wasn't his fault. She was responsible for her own feelings; she'd always known that, and this time was no different. Rae knew she had a decision to make. Stay or go. It seemed so simple, so black and white, yet there were consequences to each choice, hidden like the currents roiling beneath the smooth surface of a deep river.

She could leave Jase Van Allen behind, leave his little town and all the work she'd started as easily as buying a bus ticket. Or she could stop fighting her attraction to him.

The second choice was tempting, all the more so

because she'd already gotten a taste of how things could be between them.

Once Jase stopped trying so hard to get under her skin, Rae discovered that she truly enjoyed his dry sense of humor, his quick wit and those intense moments when he listened to her as if what she had to say was the most important thing in the world.

They'd talked all morning, laughed and bantered as if they were old friends. Except for that one tense moment by the Tilt-A-Whirl, Jase had never once done or said anything intimately suggestive.

That didn't mean she'd stopped reacting to his deep, compelling voice, or had been able to resist stealing a glance at him every now and again. Nor had she been able to ignore the way need flashed through her when she watched the grace of his body, heavy muscles moving with sleek suppleness beneath denim and cotton.

The thought of spending the rest of her life on a farm still made her feel so enclosed in an inner darkness, until she reminded herself that she had absolutely no intention of making a lifelong commitment to any man. But she had to face the fact that she wanted to spend time with Jase—in and out of bed.

And why shouldn't she? Rae wondered, resting her elbows on the table and dropping her chin into her palms. Why not have a short, intense fling with Jase? He hadn't expressed any long-term interest in her, so who would be hurt if she gave in to her desire—and his—for the few days she would be around? The more she thought about it, the less sense it made for her to keep pushing him away when they both wanted the same thing.

Besides, she'd come to Current to do a job, and the simple truth was, she just couldn't see herself leaving it half done or running away from a man just because he'd appealed to her so quickly and deeply.

Right or wrong, the decision was made and Rae searched the crowd for Jase, eager to tell him. . . .

What? And when? Should she drop it into the lunch conversation so she could watch him choke on his hot dog? Or maybe while he was looking over the bulls. She could just hear herself. *That one looks like a good breeder, Jase, and by the way, I've decided to go to bed with you.*

She caught sight of him just then, and a bubble of hysterical laughter lodged in the back of her throat. She watched him thread his way through the tables and by the time he got to her, tall and vital and handsome as sin, she'd gone absolutely speechless.

The ease she'd found in his company had burned to ash in the fire that had ignited inside her. She'd given herself the freedom to act on her desire for Jase, and just knowing that seemed to have intensified her yearnings a hundredfold.

He started to unload a cafeteria tray, and Rae concentrated almost desperately on the array of food as he set it out on the table. She didn't dare look him in the eyes until she'd gotten some control over herself.

"I actually managed to find something you didn't meet this morning," he said, dropping into the chair next to her.

He slid a thick square of cheese pizza in front on her, but she couldn't even begin to imagine choking it down past the lump in her throat.

"I thought you were hungry," Jase said, startling her into an ill-advised glance at his face.

Rae felt herself flushing and looked down at the table, suddenly shy and tongue-tied.

"If you don't want pizza, there's just about every other food you can imagine here. Tell me what you want and I'll get it for you."

"This is fine," she managed, pulling off a corner of the crust and putting it in her mouth. She had to wash it down with a long drink of soda, but once it hit her empty stomach, it seemed to help.

Her head stopped spinning, her pulse steadied and her stomach rumbled, demanding more food. A companionable silence fell between them, broken only by the rattle of ice and the crinkle of paper as they sated at least one of their bodily desires.

Jase finally sat back with a sigh, and Rae could feel him watching her. Self-conscious again, she pushed away the remains of her pizza and toyed with her soda straw, jabbing it into the ice in her paper cup and studying the results as if she'd created a masterpiece.

"Why didn't you bring your camera today?"

He'd startled her, as much for breaking the tense silence between them as for the question itself. "I didn't want to lug it around," she said, so amazed at herself she totally lost her unexpected attack of shyness.

For the first time since she'd taken her very first picture, she didn't have a camera near to hand and she hadn't even noticed. Jase was *that* distracting to her. If he could take her mind off photography that completely, it would be better to get him out of her system now than to always wonder what she'd missed.

She'd made the right decision, Rae realized, and for the second time in less than an hour she felt a tremendous sense of relief.

"It's just that I don't think I've seen you without your camera since you got to town," Jase said.

Rae sat back in her chair, and even managed to look into Jase's eyes without falling to pieces. "I've been to dozens of fairs like this, Jase. I didn't see any reason to take pictures of one more."

"Not even of your prize-winning jars of apricot jam?"

"It's your mother's jam, and it hasn't won any prizes yet." But deep inside she knew it would. Her grandmother had won every year she'd entered it.

"The judging should be getting underway right after the parade."

"Parade?"

Jase watched Rae's eyes light up and he couldn't help but smile. Her mood had been so up and down in the last couple of hours, it lifted his heart just to know he'd found something that pleased her.

She tipped her head to one side, a slow smile curving her generous mouth as she figured out that the tinny music growing louder was the valiant effort of a high-school band.

An all too familiar heat rushed through Jase. He knew if he didn't look away he'd have to stay put for a while—that or ignore the people who might notice something if he stood up. He'd almost managed to get his sense of arousal under control, until Rae jumped out of her chair and grabbed his arm.

"C'mon, Jase, I've always been a sucker for parades."

"I wish I'd known that," he muttered, getting gingerly to his feet.

"I used to look forward to the Fourth of July and Thanksgiving," Rae continued, oblivious to his comment. "Before—" Before my mother died, she'd been about to say, then decided it would only sadden them both. "When I was little we used to go into town, and there would be people and music. It was so exciting after being stuck out on the farm day after day."

"Every kid loves parades, no matter where they live," Jase said, stung by her evident dislike for his way of life.

Rae blushed and dropped her hand from his arm. "I guess I've never outgrown it."

He felt like a heel for destroying her enjoyment. He started to gather up their trash, glancing at her when she just stood there, staring longingly toward the midway. She couldn't see anything from there, not with all the people crowded along the parade route, but she didn't make a move to leave him.

"Give me a hand or we'll miss the whole thing," he said, his heart lurching when her smile blazed back to life.

They each took an armload of trash and dumped it into the huge metal barrels provided, then started across the picnic area. Rae hurried ahead, her child-like impatience belying the graceful sway of her hips, the slide of firm muscles under the satiny skin of her long, bare legs.

Jase hung back to enjoy the show, laughing when she frowned at him over her shoulder, then stopped and turned, planting her hands on her hips. When he caught up with her, she took his hand and pulled him toward a small space between two of the game tents.

Their fingers just naturally twined together, and Jase felt something shift inside him, as if the world had been spinning just slightly off-kilter and had slipped back into place when Rae held his hand. It felt right, so absolutely perfect that panic raced through him.

She hadn't meant anything by it, he told himself,

except to hurry him along. He could tell by looking at her face that she didn't even realize her fingers were still curled around his. He squeezed her hand for just a second, memorizing the feel of their palms pressed together, then let go.

He didn't know what had changed inside him, but he couldn't bear to let her pull away first again. Better to relinquish the warm, wonderful feel of her touch than to have it wrenched away when she realized she'd let things go too far.

Rae pretended she didn't notice when his hand dropped from hers, but she felt so empty now that they weren't touching anymore. She wanted to grab his hand and hold it tight between both of hers, but she resisted.

It would be a purely selfish act and she'd already been contrary enough, pushing Jase away time and time again. And now, out of the blue, she was holding his hand. He must be so confused, it was no wonder he'd started to be cautious.

His caution wouldn't last long, though. Rae still had no idea when or where she would let Jase know she'd changed her mind about their relationship, but she refused to worry about it anymore. It would happen when the time was right.

Nine

Jase's left hand gripped the steering wheel so tightly his knuckles ached. His left arm and shoulder were stiff and sore and his right leg was cramping up from pressing on the gas pedal for the better part of two hours. His right arm had gone numb long ago, but he didn't move an inch for fear of disturbing the woman sleeping against his right side. He hardly dared to breathe, for that matter, and although he was exhausted there was little chance he'd fall asleep himself. Not in his current state of arousal.

As if having Rae nestled into him weren't enough, Jase dropped his face into her hair and inhaled. Pleasure poured through him, as much from the heady scent of her as from the feel of her curled so trustingly close.

He'd invited her to spend the day with him, hoping she would relax and just enjoy his company—and realize how good they could be together. Even in his wildest dreams, it hadn't ended this well, though, and he cautioned himself not to read too much into the situation.

She was exhausted; that was the only reason she'd accepted the offer of his shoulder as a pillow. So why did he need to read more into it?

Because, he answered himself, something had changed today. He was probably setting himself up for a huge disappointment, yet he couldn't help but notice that Rae had seemed more at ease when they'd left the fairgrounds, almost as if she'd put all her doubts to rest. She had barely objected when he pulled her across the seat and urged her head onto his shoulder.

He'd only wanted her near, and now he couldn't stop thinking about his hand, resting just under the tempting curve of her breast, her breath bathing his neck, and the warm, sleepy weight of her cuddled close to his side.

He turned down the last stretch of road toward

Norge Farm, thanking God they were almost home before too many days of unsatisfied need had him coming up with some crazy idea he wasn't strong enough to resist—like pulling over to the side of the road and kissing her awake. She'd responded so passionately to his kisses before . . .

Jase blew out a harsh breath and shook his head to banish that idea.

He pulled into the farm yard—which wasn't easy to do one-handed—and stopped the truck by the row house. He hated to awaken Rae, but he had to or go crazy. He nudged her, whispering her name.

She only nestled her head into the hollow of his shoulder, mumbling something that got lost in the feel of her lips nuzzling his neck.

Jase half-turned toward her, patting her cheek to awaken her. But he couldn't resist the softness of her skin, and the pat turned into a caress. Rae's sleepy sigh was too close to a sound of passion for his comfort. She moved her hand to brush at her face, then let it drop—right into his lap. The heat of her soft flesh over his hardness inflamed a desire that was nearly impossible to control.

Instead Jase froze. He knew he should move and end the agony of unsatisfied need, but there was pleasure in her innocent touch, too. He couldn't resist indulging himself, though he couldn't stand it for more than a few seconds and still keep his sanity.

"Rae," he whispered hoarsely. "Wake up."

Rae didn't want to come out of the warm, safe cocoon of sleep, so it took a moment for her to realize that her sudden peace of mind had a direct connection to the fact that she was all but wrapped in Jase's arms. Even then she didn't move.

The dim light and the haziness of sleep freed her

of all her reservations. She tipped her head back and met Jase's eyes, cupping her fingers around the hard ridge of flesh beneath her palm. He groaned and caught her wrist, but he didn't pull her hand away.

Instead, his mouth crashed down over hers, then gentled almost instantly. But after all the days of denial, Rae didn't want gentle. She slipped her fingers into the thick hair at the nape of his neck and poured herself into the kiss, body and soul.

Jase pulled back, only far enough to whisper, "Are you sure?"

His voice was rough with need, and Rae felt her own desire flare even higher. She was touched that he would put her welfare first.

She turned to face him—as much as she was able in the cramped quarters of the truck. "I'm sure."

Jase groaned and buried his face in the hollow of her throat. She arched her neck, gave herself up to the magic of his lips.

His teeth nipped her earlobe and waves of sensation shimmered over her skin. He claimed her mouth again in a kiss that made her heart flutter against her ribs. Muscles low and deep inside her quivered, clenching in helpless pleasure when his hands grazed the sides of her breasts, then locked around her hips in a vain effort to mold her against him.

He made a wordless sound of frustration, locking his arm around her waist. His other hand fumbled toward the buttons of her shirt, but Rae gently fended it off, then held it tight until he understood that she wanted him to stop.

Another kind of fire joined the one already raging in Jase's veins. He sat back against the seat, plowing his hands through his hair, hard enough to hurt. The pain helped him get a tiny measure of control—

which he badly needed if he were to keep his hands off her now.

"I thought you were sure," he rasped, trying not to make it sound like the accusation it was.

Rae traced the line of his jaw, instantly sorry for the tension she felt there. "I am sure," she said quietly. "I just . . . This isn't . . ." *This isn't what I had in mind.* But she couldn't say that, any more than she could say that she wanted this moment to be special, something she would always remember. And cherish. She didn't want Jase to get the wrong idea.

Rae exhaled heavily, hating the fact that she had to consider the future when all she wanted was to let go and enjoy the moment.

"Not here, is that what you're trying to say?" he asked.

"Not here," she echoed, flooded with such relief and gratitude that she had to squeeze her eyes shut against the tears that threatened to flow. "Thank you for understanding."

Jase grabbed her hand at the same time his door squeaked open. "I should have figured it out sooner, Rae." He pulled her out of the truck, then pressed her up against it. "It's just that I can't seem to keep my hands off you. I don't know what it is you do to me . . ."

The rest of his comment was lost as his mouth found hers again. Rae lifted to her toes, wrapped her arms around his neck and met him halfway, molding her body to his. She melted into his long, hard body, thrilled to the feel of his hands caressing her back and lower to cup her bottom and pull her tight into the vee of his thighs.

Jase tore his mouth away, pressing his forehead to hers. "I don't think this is the bed you had in mind," he whispered, thumping his fist on the side of the pickup. "But if we don't go inside, it's the only one you're going to get."

Rae looked over her shoulder, then laughed tightly. "Maybe if you put the tailgate down."

Jase bit back a curse as he swung her up into his arms and strode toward the house. How, he wondered, was he supposed to keep a rein on his need when everything Rae did and said pushed him closer to the point of total and absolute desperation? Even as that thought burned through his mind, she nuzzled her mouth against the pulse thundering in his throat.

Jase stumbled, letting her feet fall to the wood of the porch. She tipped her face up to his, their mouths met and clung as they started a slow, sensual dance into the house and up the stairs. A trail of discarded clothing marked their path, each patch of bare floor coinciding with a patch of skin bared and the time spent exploring, discovering the textures and sensitivities uncovered.

Jase pulled her through a door, and Rae caught a glimpse of dark paneling, wide windows accented with burgundy and forest green. Then he became her entire world.

His scent spiced every breath she drew into her lungs, his heart pounded in time with hers and his touch was everywhere at once. Pleasure shot through her. Need danced along her nerve endings and throbbed through her veins.

She held Jase's glittering gaze as she slipped the thin satin straps of her bra off her shoulders, one at a time. Never looking away, he traced the edge of one lace cup, then slipped a finger beneath.

Rae closed her eyes as he pulled the bra away, the

cool air replaced by the warmth of his hand, then a moister heat and the softness of his tongue teasing her nipple. She flexed her fingers into the hard muscles of his shoulders, arching into him at the same time.

Jase tore his mouth free. She was so responsive, so passionate he felt like he'd explode if he didn't take it slower. Rae didn't seem inclined to let him.

Her fingers curled beneath the waistband of his jeans, the light scoring of her nails causing his stomach to contract and shudder. She drew him toward the bed and his heart tripped at the sensuous smile on her face, the way her eyelids half-shielded her eyes. His zipper rasped down, sounding almost loud in the tense silence. He stilled her hands and sat beside her on the bed, reaching over to cup her face.

She nestled her cheek into the palm of his hand, then her mouth, searing his skin. Jase stifled a groan and the sudden flare of sexual hunger that had inspired it. Thinking about what he had to do helped.

"Are you protected?" he asked, hating the necessity of it when he saw how Rae withdrew from him, physically and emotionally. But it would be best for them both to be sure.

"I don't make a habit of"—she waved a hand around the room, then said helplessly—"this."

Jase dropped his head to his chest for a moment in unspeakable relief. That she didn't tumble into bed with every man she met was further proof that she felt something for *him*.

"Could you take care of it?" she asked almost shyly.

He nodded. Though a part of him would have been thrilled to know she might carry his child, their relationship was much too new to either risk that possibility or to deal with the ramifications of even thinking it.

Fortunately, thinking wasn't going to be a problem for long. Once Rae made up her mind, she didn't easily change it. Jase had already learned that about her, and it seemed that giving in to her desire was no different.

She turned into him, suddenly enough to take him by surprise. He fell backwards with her on top of him, a warm, welcome weight. Her breasts crushed against his bare chest, her eyes met his, the bright blue of the hottest flame, as she threaded her fingers into the hair at his temples. Jase let the fire of her gaze consume him.

Rae wanted to just let go, to let the incredible depth of her passion for Jase carry her beyond her final reservations. She soon discovered that he would be satisfied with nothing less than wringing every second of pleasure he could from their joining.

He dispensed with the last of their clothing, then started her on a slow, torturous rise toward fulfillment. But Rae was not content to lie back and just take. She wanted to give, too, so much.

His mouth brushed hers and she met him hungrily, savoring the tastes and textures, giving in to the dark lure of desire and letting all other concerns fall away. She broke the kiss and ran her hands through the dark, springy hair covering his chest. Her eyes held his, watching every tiny nuance of his enjoyment as she discovered the feel of him, heated skin over hard muscles that quivered with her touch. Her nails skimmed across his nipples and he threw his head back. A groan that sounded like it came all the way from his toes tore through him and Rae couldn't help but smile.

"Two can play that game," Jase rasped.

He dropped his lips to the shallow cleft in her chin, then trailed them down the line of her throat and lower. Rae sucked in a breath when his cheeks, stubbled with a day's growth of beard, scraped between her breasts, setting off shivers that warred with the heat of his mouth against her skin.

He stopped suddenly, sat up and straddled her, running his hands over her ribs and across her belly. Thinking he meant to tickle her, Rae covered his hands with hers. But when she saw his face, her laughter faded away.

"You're so beautiful," he said, gently pushing her hands open so he could continue his tender exploration. The look in his eyes bordered on reverence, and he touched her so lovingly that tears came to her own eyes.

What little protection she'd tried to maintain around her heart melted away, and she reached blindly for him.

Jase stretched out beside her and folded her into his arms. Her blood seemed to ignite with the feel of him against her, and she felt so empty, so needy. She wanted to take him into her, fast and savage, anything to end the desperate need clawing at her.

He only shackled her wrists in one strong hand and held them against the mattress above her head, loving her with his mouth and his body. He brought her to the brink of release and held her there until she was too weak to even beg, then he joined his body to hers in one long, slow slide that catapulted her over the edge of oblivion.

She didn't feel Jase let go of her wrists, but it wouldn't have mattered anyway. Rapture exploded through her body, an avalanche of sensation so sharp and bright it took a monumental effort to wrap her arms around Jase as he moved above and within her, so strong and handsome she had to shut her eyes before she wept with the pleasure he gave her.

Jase drank the hoarse cries from her lips and gave himself up to the demand raging inside him. He buried himself deep one last time, letting the incredible euphoria take him until the room spun and the only stability was Rae. Heart racing, struggling for breath, he slipped to the side, folding her into his arms and holding on for dear life as he slowly returned to reality. Well, this was better than reality, considering the woman curled so warm and soft by his side.

Rae sighed softly, snuggling against him. Within seconds her breath had evened out into the rhythm of deep sleep. Jase was thankful she didn't realize how tightly he was holding her, because he couldn't bear to let her go yet.

Even though his body was sated, there were other needs deep inside him, needs that were not so easily satisfied. He gazed down at the woman in his arms, marveling at the treasure he held close to his heart.

Rae was so lovely, vulnerable yet strong, giving herself sweetly one moment, then demanding everything he had to give the next. She'd surrendered to her desire, yet in that surrender, she'd mastered him.

He was helpless to resist the wonderful contradictions of her, the beauty and passion, the completely entrancing woman who had turned his life totally upside down. His last thought as sleep stole over him was that he had no intention of letting her go. Somehow he'd convince Rae Morgan to marry him, no matter what it took.

Ten

Rae awoke feeling absolutely marvelous, content all the way to her toes. Even before she opened her eyes, she decided to enjoy it for as long as it lasted. She couldn't remember the last time she'd just relaxed and enjoyed herself, but she intended to spend her day doing exactly that. No cameras, no wondering about tomorrow or next week or whether she'd ever see her photographs on display in some gallery or gracing a magazine cover.

No agonizing over where her affair with Jase was headed or why she'd given in in the first place. No dwelling on a past she couldn't change and a future she didn't want to. For the moment, she was right where she wanted to be and she refused to ruin it by analyzing it to death.

She stretched, groaning as long unused muscles ached a little. The sheet grazed her breasts, still tender from the night's lovemaking, sending faint tremors through her, erotic echoes of the pleasure Jase had given her only hours before.

Rae smiled and let herself enjoy the way her body quickened at the mere reminder of him. She would have turned to Jase to satisfy the sudden craving that had leaped to life inside her, but he'd left hours ago. And the memory of how made her smile grow even wider.

Jase had awakened her to say good-bye, but the light kiss he'd dropped on her lips had deepened into hello and then they'd gotten to know each other very well. Again. She could still smell him on the sheets—and on her own skin—the unique spice of him not quite masked by soap and shaving cream. She'd never known a fragrance could be so erotic. Rae drew in a deep breath, not sure if her head swam because of Jase's scent or if she was hyperventilating.

She knew one thing, though, she needed to get her feet back on the ground, figuratively and literally, before she lost her head. Before she could change her mind, she jumped out of bed in one quick motion, hissing in a breath as the morning air instantly chilled her heated skin.

Hoping for a steaming shower, Rae tossed on her clothes and headed for the row house. Or maybe, she mused, she'd try the century-old sauna. It had been built by the original Scandinavian settlers who'd founded the farm, but Jase's father had refurbished it with state-of-the-art workings. It sounded heavenly, and by the time she opened the door to the little house where she'd been staying, she had made up her mind to have the sauna *and* the shower. And then she'd pick a book from the small selection in Jase's room and settle on the porch swing to waste the rest of the morning.

Making yourself right at home, a little voice mocked, but she refused to listen. This was supposed to be her vacation and if she chose to spend it being lazy, and wonderfully self-indulgent, that was her choice.

Rae stopped on the small porch and took a deep breath, hoping she didn't have to defend her actions to Chrissy as hard as she'd had to defend them to herself. When she stepped inside, though, she knew immediately that Chrissy wasn't there. Not only did the little house feel empty, but her friend's bright pink luggage wasn't strewn about the small living room. And then she saw the note, propped on the coffee table.

Rae breathed a sigh of relief, but her heart sank, and dread set in as she unfolded the single sheet of paper and read the few lines.

Something came up in Chicago and I didn't think it would be fair to pull you away from Jase just when . . . Well, I'm not sure what's happening. I don't think you are either, but you really should find out. Anyway, I'll be back for you in two weeks. Don't worry. I'll clear it with Dad.

Underneath the elaborate curliqued signature was a P.S.

Don't waste time being angry with me. I only want what's best for you.

By the time she finished the note, Rae could barely see through the red haze clouding her eyes. She felt like her head was going to explode, she was filled with so much anger. And panic.

She whirled around and raced to the front door, though she had no idea what she'd do when she got there. She only knew she wasn't going to be trapped here by some romantic whim of Chrissy's.

But she was.

Rae sank down on the front step and cradled her head in her hands. Of all the thoughtless things to do. Something came up in Chicago, hah! Chrissy was running away from Kurt Van Linden and she had the gall to claim she'd deserted Rae for her own good? What kind of friend did that? she wondered, not caring whether it was logical or not.

All that mattered was finding a way to leave Norge Farm before Jase got home and her resolve disappeared. Maybe she could borrow one of the farm trucks, or call Kurt and see if he'd give her a ride to town. From there, she might be able to catch a bus or rent a car.

But even if that were possible, Rae realized she couldn't just take off—not after last night. And not just for Jase's sake.

Long before Chrissy had decided to force the issue, Rae had already made up her mind to relax and enjoy her time with Jase. Instead of panicking, she ought to be overjoyed that she had an extra week.

So why did she feel as if she'd jumped into water a mile deep with no dry land in sight?

If Chrissy hadn't gone back to Chicago, Jase would have kissed her for adding seven more days to his time with Rae. Last night had been incredible, but he'd known Rae would have doubts in the bright light of day, and he'd been half afraid he would come home to an empty house. However uncertain Rae might feel, Chrissy had made it impossible for her to simply take off in the red convertible.

Instead, Rae had funneled her energy into more traditional areas. The house was spotless, and the meal he'd come home to smelled heavenly.

It tasted like sawdust. Jase choked it down for appearance's sake, but he couldn't enjoy anything with Rae sitting across the table from him, fidgeting and picking at her food as if she wanted to be anywhere else than the kitchen that had always been the heart of Jase's home.

And he had to admit that it made him uncomfortable to have her cooking and cleaning for him. It wasn't that he didn't like the thought of her waiting to welcome him after a long day of work. But he knew it wasn't what Rae wanted.

"If I had known Chrissy was leaving, I'd have made sure you had something to drive so you wouldn't be stuck here alone all day."

Rae's head jerked up and her troubled blue eyes met his. "I managed to keep busy," she said softly.

Jase found himself looking at the top of her head again, and his heart twisted. He hadn't meant to make her unhappy. "The house looks great, Rae, and it's wonderful to have a hot, fresh meal after a week of leftovers, but I don't expect you to spend your vacation slaving away for my comfort."

"It was no trouble," she said, then spent a silent moment meticulously separating the different foods on her plate so that none of them touched the other.

Jase realized he was holding his fork so tightly his fingers ached. He took a drink of water, a few deep breaths, but he couldn't relax. His mind would never be at ease until Rae's was. "What's wrong?"

She glanced up at him, then away. Very carefully, she put her fork down on the edge of her plate. "Last night was wonderful," she said, her voice low, almost inaudible.

"I wouldn't change a second of it."

Rae blushed, her fingers smoothing the already immaculate tablecloth. "Neither would I, Jase."

"But?"

She heaved a deep sigh. "But I think we need to get some things cleared up before we go any further. I'm only going to be here for two more weeks. I need to know you understand that."

And there it was, Jase thought, the disclaimer he'd been expecting. *You can only have so much of me for so long* was what she meant. He should probably count himself fortunate that she hadn't decamped with Chrissy, but somehow he didn't feel lucky to have her sit there and place a time limit on their relationship just when he couldn't imagine the rest of his life without her in it. And he'd be damned if he agreed to it.

"Why don't we just take it a day at a time and see what happens?"

"I know what's going to happen, Jase. In two weeks I'll go back to Chicago and you'll stay here."

"Norge Farm isn't that far from Chicago," he said tightly. "We can see each other on weekends."

Rae dropped her hands into her lap so he wouldn't see them trembling. When she had rehearsed this little speech in her mind, she had seen Jase accepting that they would have two wonderful weeks together, then go their separate ways. She should have known he wouldn't make it that easy on her. From the moment they'd met he'd been pushing her for more than she could give. "I work weekends."

"Then I'll come down during the week. We can't just spend two weeks together and then say good-bye before we know—"

"What are you saying?" she demanded harshly.

Jase shrugged, though Rae could tell that he was getting angry. "There's something between us, Rae, something deeper than a few nights between the sheets. Just because you have to go back to work doesn't mean we should call it quits. Chicago's not a million miles away."

One by one, Rae felt her muscles unlock, and she breathed a sigh of relief. For a second she'd thought he was talking about something permanent, maybe even marriage! Thank God he wasn't, she thought, as the urge to race for the door subsided. "Well, right now I'm living in Chicago, Jase, but I'm not going to be there for much longer and I have no idea where

I am going to end up living." She held up a hand when he tried to speak. "What really matters is that your life is here, on this farm. You wouldn't be happy anywhere else and . . ."

"And you don't think you could be happy here," he finished when she couldn't. "Why not?"

Rae shoved her chair back and got up, pacing across the wide kitchen. "I grew up on a farm, Jase."

"I already know that."

She leaned against the doorjamb and took a deep breath of the freedom on the other side of the screen door. It would be so easy to walk out, so tempting to escape these walls that seemed to close in on her. She could lose herself in the velvety night so she wouldn't have to face the darkness inside herself.

But she knew the barriers around her had been built of something much stronger than wood and plaster. They'd been built out of her own fears and insecurities, her belief that she would never live up to her own expectations. Or that she would live down to her father's.

"Rae?"

For one brief second she thought about putting on a smile, asking him to just forget she'd ever started this. *Begging*, if she had to.

But Jase deserved the truth. And maybe it would help him understand why she couldn't be the woman he wanted her to be.

"My mother's name was Lynn Morgan. She was beautiful and sweet, Jase. I remember . . ." Rae took a moment to force down the lump in her throat. There was nothing she could do about the ache in her heart. "She made everything so much fun. Housework, cooking, canning, all the chores that could have been so tedious were games for me because of my mother. We used to sing and laugh all day." Her voice broke and she tipped her head back, blinking furiously. "Until my father came in from the fields or the barns or wherever he'd been working.

"I'll never understand why she stayed with a man who went out of his way to make her miserable, but she did."

"Maybe there was a side to their relationship you didn't see," Jase offered quietly. "Maybe she loved him."

Rae didn't realize she'd been holding her breath until it exploded out of her in a sound ripe with scorn. "She loved him all right. She must have or she wouldn't have stayed there and let him belittle her and blame her for everything that went wrong, real or imaginary. My mother almost died having me and then she couldn't have any more children. My father never forgave her for that. He made her life hell, all because she couldn't give him a son."

Jase stared at the rigid line of Rae's back. His throat ached for the little girl who hadn't been able to understand why the father she loved didn't seem to want her. He yearned to put his arms around the woman who couldn't see that her father had been the real loser, but it wasn't in his power to heal that wound. "It sounds like he's still making you miserable, Rae."

She stiffened. "I left that part of my life behind a long time ago."

"Did you?" His chair scraped back and Rae glanced over her shoulder, thankful to see he'd only moved away from the table so he could stretch his long legs out and get comfortable. She didn't think she could stand for him to touch her at the moment, not when she felt so . . . brittle. Needy.

"Think about it, Rae," he pressed. "Aren't you still

making decisions about your life because of your father?"

"I—"

"Don't tell me," Jase said with quiet conviction. "You're the one you need to convince."

Silence fell, so thick Rae felt like she was laboring to breathe. She tried to calm herself, but it felt so good to exorcise some of the anger filling her heart, anger she thought she'd put to rest a long time ago. Obviously she hadn't.

She could still hear her father's voice as he ranted on and on, blaming all his troubles on his wife. His entire life seemed futile because he didn't have a son to work by his side, he used to say, a son who would share his burden rather than add to it. There had been a Morgan on his land for over two hundred years, and now all he had to leave behind was a daughter who would get married and take her husband's name.

On the worst days he'd made Rae feel less than worthless, but Lynn had always tried to shield her daughter, make up for the fact that she was essentially fatherless. And then she'd deserted Rae, too.

"She loved him so much she stayed with him until he wore her out. She died very suddenly one winter, of pneumonia. But I think she just let go of a life she couldn't stand to live anymore. I'll never forgive him for that."

"You don't have to forgive him, Rae, just stop letting him ruin your life."

Rae grimaced at the patronizing, pitying tone of Jase's voice. She turned around and faced him, chin high. "I didn't tell you this to make you feel sorry for me, Jase. I only want you to understand why I feel the way I do. In two weeks I'm going back to Chicago so I can get on with my life."

"You have a strange definition of getting on with your life when all you're doing is running away. You'll never put the past where it belongs until you face it."

She wrapped her arms around her waist and hunched her shoulders. "Stick to farming, Jase. I don't need a psychiatrist."

"I only want what's best for you."

"What is there to gain by going back?" she demanded.

Jase leaned his chair back against the counter with a nonchalance he didn't come close to feeling. "Peace?"

Rae shook her head. "You just don't understand, and why should you? Norge Farm is your home—a real home.

"My so-called home was like one of those houses they build for a Hollywood movie. Beautiful on the outside, white and clean and perfect, but when you go through the door there's nothing but a few two-by-fours holding it up. Nothing, Jase. Certainly no peace."

She was hurting, and Jase's heart went out to her, but he had no intention of letting her deny them a future because she couldn't put the past to rest. "So how do you plan on living while you're traipsing around the country?"

Rae winced at the bitterness and sarcasm in his deep voice, but she'd expected it. Her first instinct was to go to him, rest her head on his shoulder and forget about the day they had to part. But her conscience wouldn't allow that. "I have plans—"

"Like what, Rae?" he said with quiet vehemence.

"What's so important that you would sacrifice everything else in your life?"

That you would sacrifice me. Jase hadn't said those words aloud but Rae heard them all the same. Guilt and regret crushed down on her. "I shouldn't have gotten involved with you," she said heavily. "It wasn't fair to you when I knew I would be leaving."

Jase felt his blood run cold. He knew he could overcome her memories, given time. He wasn't so sure he could fight the life she'd made for herself in Chicago, her job and her friends. Male friends, he couldn't help but think. "You haven't answered my question, Rae. What's so important that you would sacrifice everything else for it?"

"You wouldn't understand, Jase."

"Try me."

Rae leaned back against the counter and studied him. He'd been honest with her from the first. He deserved the same from her. She blew out a long breath of air that lifted the bangs from her forehead, and dived in. "I never really knew what I wanted to do . . . past getting out of my hometown. Five minutes after I graduated from high school I got in my car and headed for Chicago, and quickly found out my diploma was all but worthless. In my hometown, girls were encouraged to take home ec and sewing classes, so I was prepared to be a farm wife or a waitress."

"I know farm wife isn't high on your list of preferred careers," Jase said with a wry twist of his full mouth. "So I assume you got a job waitressing."

"I worked as a cocktail waitress at night."

"Short skirt and all?"

She grinned, grateful that he seemed to be taking

everything so well. So far. "I'll leave that up to your imagination."

Jase groaned and rolled his eyes in wordless appreciation.

"Anyway, I took some classes at a small college. And then one day I walked into a classroom where Chrissy's father was teaching." She smiled and her eyes took on a faraway look. "He saw something in me. By the end of that semester I was working for him. Chrissy and I became friends from the moment we met and that meant almost as much to me."

She focused on him again. "I can't even begin to tell you what it was like, Jase. All of a sudden I was living in a big city with a million things to choose from, I had someone who saw potential in me and a person who was like a sister. Almost a family."

Jase didn't want to hear any more about her wonderful life in Chicago, but he knew he had to get the whole story before he could understand what he was up against. "It must have been great, Rae, but you still haven't told me what you were doing."

Her brow furrowed in puzzlement.

"What kind of classes were you taking?"

"Oh! Photography. I thought you'd figured that out already since you kept asking questions about my camera."

Jase sent her a crooked grin. "I guess I should have."

She turned serious all of a sudden, almost shy. "I want to be a photographer more than anything, Jase. When Chrissy heard about Kurt's ad—"

"That's why you came to town?" he asked, an incredulous smile lighting his face. "You've been chasing poor Kurt around to document his mail-order marriage in pictures? What if he's got you in mind for the bride?"

"Kurt knows all about why I've been 'chasing' him," she retorted. "I swore him to secrecy because I didn't want people posing whenever they saw me. And I happen to know he has someone else in mind for the bride."

"Chrissy?"

"He swore me to secrecy," she repeated, grinning when Jase frowned at her. "And that's beside the point. I would never use someone for my own selfish ends. That's why I'm telling you all this now, so you won't get false ideas about . . . us."

Jase couldn't meet her steady gaze and doubt that she had told him the absolute truth—as she saw it. "So you want to be a photographer. What kind?"

She shrugged. "Art photography, photojournalism, freelance assignments . . . I'd do almost anything as long as I can have a camera in my hand."

"Chasing celebrities around for the tabloids?"

She wrinkled her nose in distaste. "Even if I could see my way clear to intruding on a person like that, I don't have the killer instinct it takes to get photos of someone's facelift scars. And anyway, I hear movie stars have taken to punching the paparazzi lately."

Jase couldn't help but smile. "I don't think I'd take it kindly if some high-paid actor broke your nose."

Rae smiled softly. "I'd have to say that art photography is my first love. Like the pictures I took of your pasture," she added when he looked puzzled. "But I have to eat, which means I would have to take assignments until I can establish myself. I'll have to pick up and travel at the drop of a hat, Jase."

"And what if it takes you the next thirty years to get established? Or what if you never do? Are you willing to give up ever having a home and family for something that might never happen?"

She scowled at him, but he didn't care. He'd meant to be blunt. "Have you ever heard of Morris Fremont?" she asked tightly.

Jase whistled through his teeth. "Who hasn't? You can't go anywhere without seeing one of his photographs."

"Exactly. He's only taken three apprentices. The first two have gone on to become famous, and I'm the third."

"So he's Chrissy's father," Jase mused, almost to himself. That certainly put a wrinkle in his logic. Still . . . "It's all well and good for Morris Fremont to assure you that you'll do well but it's your life on the line, Rae. What makes you so sure you'll make it?"

"Because I want it so bad." She shoved away from the counter, her back rigid. "Because I'm willing to work as hard and as long as it takes." She began to pace again, clearly agitated. "Do you think I've never been rejected? It only makes me work harder, Jase. I can't give up; something inside of me just won't let me."

She whirled around to face him again. "That's what I'm trying to tell you. I'll make whatever sacrifice it takes in order to reach my goal and if I look back in thirty years and regret it, I'll deal with that, too."

Jase heard her out and made a silent vow. He was going to make her want him that much—no matter how long it took. Not matter what he had to do.

Eleven

Rae opened the door to the sauna and stepped inside. A soft cloud of steam enveloped her, but as it cleared she saw a daisy chain lying on the wooden bench, and her heart skipped a beat. It had been left there by Jase, of course, and so recently the daisies hadn't begun to wilt from the heat yet.

She settled on the bench, carefully pulling the flowers into her lap and running her fingers over the delicate leaves and petals. Strangely comforted, she tipped her head back against the wall and closed her eyes, trying to relax.

It had been a rough morning. Taking photos of Kurt in town should have been pleasant and easy; her work had always centered her, and she knew she'd done some of her best work ever that morning. The photos were going to be so poignant, and very powerful, but Rae felt like she was taking advantage of a situation she'd had a hand in causing. It had been her idea to come here, after all, and now Kurt was paying the price for her career aspirations.

The moment she had focused her camera on his eyes, a gorgeous blue now saddened by sorrow, she had seen why every woman he met knew he'd already given his heart away. She'd offered not to use the pictures, but he'd insisted she go ahead. It was what she'd come to Current for, but she still felt sad.

Jase's sweet gesture lightened her heart. How, she wondered, did he always know what she needed before she knew herself? It awed her, humbled her that he cared so much, and it made her feel guilty.

In the two days since their conversation, he'd been careful not to crowd her. Yet she had purposely kept her agenda a secret. After spending the night in Jase's arms, it gave her a sense of freedom to take off without telling him where she was going.

In light of his patience and tenderness, it seemed petty and resentful of her to hold back. Yet she was helpless to change the way she felt, even though she'd come to realize that her own fears and insecurities held her prisoner, not Jase.

He'd been attentive, but not smothering. He never failed to let her know how much he enjoyed having her around in a dozen little ways, from simple, touching gifts like making a daisy chain for her or listening to her when she talked. No one had ever just listened to her, except her mother—and that had been so long ago she had forgotten what it felt like.

If he was mounting a campaign to win her heart, he was going about it the right way. She loved knowing she could turn to him any time of the day or night and he would be there, willing to talk or make love or just hold her. Rae knew she ought to cut her losses and leave Norge Farm before she got in over her head, but she couldn't bring herself to do it yet. She found so much pleasure with Jase, and she knew she brought him pleasure. She didn't want to deny either of them that joy.

"You all right in there?"

Rae smiled at the sound of Jase's deep voice but she didn't open her eyes or lift her head. Nor did she think the shiver chasing over her skin was due to the fact that he'd opened the door and let in cool air.

She didn't fight the familiar heat, just let it slam

through her blood and settle into aching points of need. Her pulse began to drum in her ears and tingle throughout her body in a surge of restless energy. Her toes curled and she reached her arms over her head and stretched languorously, enjoying the way Jase could make her feel so vital and alive.

"Rae?"

"I was just about to come out." She sat up, grimacing as she caught sight of her sweat darkened T-shirt and bike shorts. She pulled the soggy cotton away from her stomach. "If you can stand me like this."

Jase grinned. "My only objection is that I didn't help you get that way." He reached out and caught her fingers, pulling her to her feet. "But I'd like a chance to later on."

"What's wrong with right now?"

The smile faded from his tempting mouth and the humor in his sexy dark eyes was replaced by the intense, smoldering look that always made her blood pump in hot spurts through her veins.

"I should get back to the north pasture." But all that moved were his eyes, dropping to her mouth.

Rae moistened her lips, suddenly dry beneath the heat of his gaze.

"I know there's a hole in the fence somewhere," he said, his voice dropping lower with each word he spoke. "The cows keep getting . . . out . . . ."

"Sounds important," Rae said as she stripped off her soggy T-shirt and the athletic bra beneath.

"My horse—" Jase had to stop and clear his throat, though it didn't help much. "I left my horse saddled outside."

Jase's big body blocked the partially open door, but Rae peered over his shoulder and saw the horse standing head down, one leg cocked. "He's dozing

in the shade of that big old maple you tied him to."
She picked up the daisy chain and draped it around
her neck, shuddering a little as the stems tickled her.
"Besides, I haven't thanked you for the flowers yet."

"Jeez, Rae, you're killing me," Jase rasped. His
gaze trailed over his gift. The dark green leaves and
pristine white petals clung to her sweat-slicked ivory
skin, teased circles of darker flesh and grazed her
swollen nipples with every breath she took.

"I have just the cure," she whispered, peeling off
her skintight jogging shorts and the wisp of silk beneath.

He told himself he should walk away, prove that
he could resist her so he could look back on this
moment after she was gone and tell himself he could
live without her. His heart knew differently, though.

When—if—Rae left him, he had no doubt he'd
end up as miserable and heartsore as Kurt for a long
time. Maybe forever.

He'd be a fool to waste a moment with her.

Jase stepped forward, allowing the spring-hinged
door to fall shut behind him. Gloom enveloped them,
and before his eyes could adjust, he felt Rae's hands
slip beneath his white cotton T-shirt, sliding it up his
chest, letting her nails gently scratch over his skin.

"Stop," he groaned, tearing the shirt off in one
violent motion and pressing her palms flat against
his chest.

"You don't really want me to stop or you wouldn't
let me pull my hands free and do this."

Rae stepped close enough for her peaked nipples
to brush his chest, and when her fingers dipped below the waist of his jeans, Jase had to lock his knees
before his legs gave out.

He could do nothing about the way his muscles

jumped and shuddered. All he could do was stand there while she tormented him with her soft, maddening touch and her hot, clever mouth. That or he'd have to throw her down on the bench and—

And, as crazed as she'd made him, he might hurt her. He grabbed her wrists, held her hands out to the side and took deep, shuddering breaths. Unfortunately, the hot moist air inside the sauna, laden with Rae's scent, did little to help him regain control. Neither did her throaty laugh.

"I swear, if you don't stop, sweetheart, I'll—"

"You'll what?" Rae challenged, raising her chin and catching his gaze. She knew he'd never hurt her, despite the wild desire in his eyes. And she wanted him to take her fast, to drive everything from her mind but the here and now, the magic they created when their bodies joined and she lost track of where he left off and where she started.

Lord, how she loved being with him like this. How she loved being with him. Period.

Gently she twisted her wrists free of his grip, twined her fingers into the hair at his nape and pulled his head down to hers. A soul-deep groan tore through Jase as their mouths met. The sound vibrated into Rae and blasted through her on a wave of adrenaline that made her tingle with energy.

She reached between them and found his zipper, then slipped her hands into his loosened jeans and the briefs beneath. Her hands followed the cloth, over his tight buttocks and down his thighs, then back up.

He leaned into her and she gasped when he twisted against her, back and forth. The hair on his chest and their damp skin produced friction, and the friction produced heat. Or maybe the heat came from deep inside, where she burned for Jase.

Rae took a step forward, then another, trying to back him toward the bench. He grabbed her by the upper arms and held her in place, mumbling something against her mouth.

"Where's your sense of adventure?" she asked breathlessly. "I know the bench is narrow, but . . . We can hardly walk to the house like this."

Jase gave a pained laugh and looked down at his feet. "I can't walk anywhere like this."

Rae followed his line of sight, and burst out laughing. Jase's pants were accordioned around his ankles, just the tips of his riding boots visible beneath the faded denim. "I think I like having you at my mercy." She shoved lightly at his shoulders, chuckling when he stepped back to keep his balance, arms in the air.

His knees hit the bench and he plopped down, half dragging her on top of him. "All you had to do was ask," he said. He had planned to make love to her until she begged for release, but she seemed to want to be in charge.

Rae kissed him hard, enjoying the taste and texture of his mouth on hers. The scent of man curled around her, lightly spiced with sweat and the horse he'd been riding all morning. And arousal. He tore his mouth from hers, trailing his lips down her neck before burying his face between her breasts.

And when he drew one aching nipple into his hot mouth, she nearly screamed at the pleasure of it. She cupped his head with one hand, and found him with the other, measuring the pulsing length of him with trembling fingers.

She didn't realize she was begging until Jase tore his mouth free and crushed his cheek to her stomach, sucking in ragged breaths. "Shhh," he groaned, the rush of cool air against her heated skin coiling the need inside her even tighter. "Help me get these damn boots off or I won't be any good to either of us."

Rae knelt by his feet, grabbed one boot with both hands and tried to pull it off, to no avail.

"Damn, they're stuck." He pulled his jeans up high enough so he could lift one foot in the air. "Straddle my leg and grab the boot."

She'd no sooner turned her back to him than she felt his hands caressing her backside. Callused fingertips brushed gently over her skin, followed the line of her backbone up to the nape of her neck, then down her left side, dipping into her waist and sliding over the curve of her hip.

Ripples of heat danced away from his touch, and waves of goosebumps. The cold warred with the hot and a tingle of unbearable desire ached low inside her. "Jase," she pleaded thickly. "Please . . ."

"God, you're beautiful," he moaned hoarsely. He wrapped his arm around her hips and eased her down onto his lap, one hand sliding around to cup her.

She dropped her head forward, staring at his sundarkened hand against her pale skin. His finger dipped inside her and she moaned, then gasped when the velvet hardness of him filled her instead. Excitement shot through her in dizzying bursts of light and color, and a need so intense she felt tears trickling down her cheeks.

"Please," she whispered brokenly.

Jase soothed her and heightened her longing simultaneously, with skillful caresses and hot promises of what was to come. Her whole body tightened with erotic pleasure, her back arched and he slipped deeper inside her, driving her yet higher.

She begged him to take her fast and hard, to end the incredible combination of pain and pleasure, but he moved with agonizing slowness until she thought she would die from the rapture of it. When his hand slipped between her thighs and found her, she climaxed in one glorious instant.

Everything disappeared, everything but Jase. Ecstasy throbbed through her with every stroke of his body within hers, joy pounded on each beat of her racing pulse, filling her heart with such happiness she didn't know how she'd existed without it. Jase became her anchor, soaring into oblivion with her, then cradling her back to reality as gently as he'd driven her from it.

Rae came back to the steamy sauna to find herself slumped forward, Jase still throbbing deep within her. She wanted to say something, to thank him, but there didn't seem to be any words adequate to the magnitude of what he'd given her.

"You were wrong," she finally said, smiling at the weakness of her voice, the fact that she still hadn't caught her breath.

"How's that?" he asked, equally winded.

"You were plenty good with your boots on."

Twelve

Jase scraped some lumpy scrambled eggs out of the cast iron skillet, trying not to notice how pathetic they looked after the fluffy omelet Rae had made him for dinner last night—or how lonely the kitchen felt without her presence.

After the sauna yesterday afternoon, he and Rae had taken a very erotic shower—together. She had conjured up dinner like a culinary magician, and then they'd gone to bed.

Jase didn't even try to stop the goofy smile that made his cheeks ache, or the need that sizzled through him when he remembered how they'd spent the night. As thoroughly and satisfyingly as they'd loved each other, his body still quickened.

It should have surprised him. It didn't. He'd long since made peace with the fact that he'd never tire of Rae, either her body or her company.

Last night had only proved that yet again.

He'd never needed much sleep; he'd gotten next to none, yet his body hummed with energy. He'd lain awake, watching Rae sleep for hours, wondering what it would take to make her love him. He'd still been searching for that answer when he'd had to get up and leave her.

Jase shoved his untouched breakfast away and leaned his chair against the counter behind him, wrestling with the kernel of an idea.

After the last few weeks, there wasn't an inch of Rae's body he didn't know intimately. He could touch her just so and predict whether she'd gasp or moan, and how loud. She'd given him everything he could have wanted and more—physically.

The hours they spent together between dusk and dawn were every man's dream, but he never knew how she would react to him when he saw her again after a day apart.

And maybe, he thought, letting the front legs of his chair hit the floor with a thump, that was the problem. Every morning he got up before dawn, stealing away from Rae as if the world would end if she awoke and found him beside her. In many ways, he realized, that was exactly what he feared.

He'd let Rae define the parameters of his presence in her life because he was afraid that if she thought he was intruding, she'd panic and bolt. He'd only been making it easier for her to call what they had a passing affair rather than a developing relationship.

Well, she intended to leave anyway. So what if he pushed her a bit too hard and she took off earlier than she'd planned?

He could play it safe, Jase thought, and have a few precious days with her, followed by a lifetime of loneliness. Or take the biggest risk he'd ever taken and perhaps earn himself a lifetime with the woman he loved.

Faced with that sort of choice, there was only one decision he could make.

The first thing Rae noticed was the scent of coffee, freshly ground and mouth-watering enough to awaken her from some desperately needed sleep. She opened her eyes a little, just enough to see the pearly light of dawn through the unshaded triangle of window. Her eyes drifted shut again, but one hand automatically groped across the bed—and found it empty.

Disappointment frayed the edges of her contentment, even though she'd expected to find herself alone again. Jase always got up before dawn; it was one of the things she hated about farm life, that seven day a week, crack-of-dawn commitment that had dragged him from her side every morning.

Even though she knew it was for the best, that she

didn't dare get used to waking up to his big, warm body and irreverent smile, her heart began to ache. She shifted to her side and curled around that hurt as if she could cure it if she held on to herself tight enough. But her arms were still empty.

A shiver rippled over her skin, and though she knew it had nothing to do with temperature, Rae reached for the cover.

Her hand came back filled with something soft, but it wasn't cloth.

She opened her eyes, and realized she held a handful of rose petals. The bed was covered with them. She dropped all but one, watching them fall back to the bed—red and white and buttery yellow tumbling in the first rays of sunlight.

Rae rubbed one velvety petal, still wet from dew, between her thumb and index finger, then brought it to her nose and inhaled the scent of rose and fresh morning air. Her heart fluttered, and she smiled, even as she tried not to let Jase's latest gift get to her—or think about how she'd rather have had him there when she woke up.

"You're welcome."

She rolled onto her back and saw Jase lounging against the doorframe, arms crossed over his wide chest. Rae wanted to be angry that he'd been spying on her, but how could she with him standing there, smiling so brightly he rivaled the sunrise? And all because he'd done something he thought would please her.

She sighed and gave up trying to resist him. "How can you look so wide awake after . . ."

He raised a sun-bleached brow and his grin widened into a self-satisfied smirk.

Rae refused to blush. "Where do you find the energy to get up before dawn every morning?"

"From you. It doesn't matter how little sleep I get anymore, Rae. As long as it's with you." Jase had known what her reaction would be. He still hated watching her pull back emotionally, but he'd decided to stop pussyfooting around and he meant to stick to that resolution.

Rae watched him walk into the room, his rangy stride bringing him to the side of the bed in four steps—much faster than she was ready. She could tell something had changed in Jase. There was a watchful, expectant light in his eyes that made her wary. He looked like a cat waiting to pounce on a mouse. Not to hurt it—just to play.

He sat down on the edge of the bed, his hip nestled in the curve of her waist, and even in her cautious state, Rae had to stop herself from dragging him down beside her. Her resistance to him was fading away, and that made her even more nervous.

"So what are you going to do today?" he asked.

Her eyes shifted to the window. "I need to get some shots around town."

Rae hadn't moved an inch, yet Jase could feel the distance she'd put between them. It made him angry, at her for needing so much freedom, and at himself for giving it to her for so long. It had been foolish to let her hide from her feelings.

Or maybe there was nothing to hide from.

Jase ignored that little voice of doubt. He knew in his heart that she had to feel something for him, not just because he wanted it so desperately, but because of who she was.

If Rae had been the type of woman who indulged herself whenever the whim struck, she'd have been in his bed from the first day they'd met, when desire had sizzled between them as fast and unpredictably as heat lightning. She'd admitted she was attracted to him long before she stopped fighting herself—and she'd stopped fighting herself the day they'd spent together at the fair. He felt stupid for not figuring it out sooner, but now that he'd made the connection. . . .

"I could use a few things from town," he said, picking up her hand and toying with her slender fingers. He had to smile when she pulled free, just as he'd expected. "And I could give you a little history to go with your pictures."

Rae eased a few inches from him, just far enough so she could think, away from the warmth of his body against hers. "I'm not writing an article, Jase. And I don't want to keep you from your work."

"I don't have anything planned that can't wait."

"What about the north pasture?" Rae asked. "You never did make it back there yesterday."

Jase knew she'd deliberately tried to sidetrack him. She looked so tempting lying there tousled with sleep, a slight blush warming her cheeks, that it actually worked for a minute or two before he reminded himself what was at stake. "One of the hired hands can take care of it."

"But—"

"Look, Rae, you're mistaking commitment for confinement. I have a master's degree in finance. If I didn't want to be here, I wouldn't, but this is my home, and I love it. I count myself fortunate enough to have a career here, too."

"Finance?" she asked incredulously.

"The milk and cheese don't sell themselves," Jase pointed out patiently. "Especially not in the volume we produce. I work around the farm because I like being hands-on, but I spend about half my time in the office."

"It sounds like you're pretty busy."

"I am, but it doesn't mean I'm tied to this place, Rae. I set my own hours, just like my parents. If I want to get away for a while, I go."

She snorted rudely and sat up in bed. "And when's the last time you took a vacation?"

"I went out to Wyoming a few months ago to visit my sister Jo."

"That's where your parents are, right?"

"Yeah, and I'm sure Jo is managing to keep them entertained, even though she has a successful career and helps her husband run their ranch to boot. Apparently no one has ever told her those things can't be done at the same time."

Rae glared at him, threw the covers back and started to get out of bed.

Jase caught her wrist and held tight, though he was careful not to hurt her. He didn't let the sight of her naked body or the silkiness of her soft skin distract him, either. His bitter, accusatory words bothered him, though. "I'm sorry, Rae. Jo works harder than any two people I know. It's not fair to compare anyone with her." He almost smiled when her eyes narrowed. "She's a writer. Her husband, Chase, is an artist and they've just expanded their ranch."

"I'm sure they're very happy," Rae said, plucking at the fuzz balls on the blanket.

"They are. Ranching is just as demanding as farming, but they manage to have their careers, too."

She looked like she was going to stay put, and Jase released her wrist, but just to be safe he leaned his hand on the other side of her legs.

"I'm impressed, Jase, but you're forgetting something. Writing and painting can be done anywhere. My work won't come to me. A freelance photographer has to go wherever the story is."

Jase ran a hand back through his hair, so clearly frustrated and upset that Rae was suddenly overwhelmed with guilt.

He almost choked on his next words. "I know you're leaving, Rae. All I'm asking is for you to spend one or two days more with me."

"All right," she said in a small, apologetic voice.

"What did you say?" The first thing he'd learned about Rae was that her stubborn streak went clear through her. It surprised the hell out of him when she changed her mind.

"I said all right," she repeated. "I said I'd spend time with you and I will."

Jase wasn't about to argue with that. "All day?"

"All day," she replied. "You get to choose what we'll do."

Thirteen

Rae felt as if she were back at the county fair, without the fun parts. Not that she didn't like Norge Farm, but touring a seemingly endless series of barns filled with various farm animals hadn't been high on her list of ways to spend the day.

Jase ushered her into yet another building, and she found herself in a long concrete-floored horse barn clean enough to qualify for a hospital. She meandered down the center aisle, stopping to rest her arms on the top rail of one of the gated stalls. A pretty bay mare poked her head out and nuzzled Rae's shoulder until she rewarded her with a good scratch between the ears.

Rae didn't even feel guilty for leaving Jase's side, or for tuning out his constant chatter. It was for his own good, after all.

She'd agreed to spend the day with him, and she'd been expecting a tour of the farm—especially since she'd avoided it so far. Jase wasn't just showing her around, though. He was recruiting her to his way of life.

After her childhood, it was heartwarming to see someone so dedicated to his family and home, and the way he tried so hard to show her that Norge Farm was nothing like the place she'd grown up was touching. She'd known that the moment she'd stepped out of Chrissy's convertible, but she didn't say as much. Not only would it open a subject she'd rather leave alone, but she didn't have the heart to ruin his fun.

Neither did she want to encourage him when she knew it would be cruel to let him get his hopes up. She was leaving in a few days and that was that—if only Jase would accept it.

He said he did, but Rae knew better. He was determined to change her mind. She saw it in his eyes, heard it ringing in his voice, and felt it every time he found an excuse to touch her—which he did almost constantly.

Almost before that thought crossed her mind, she sensed his presence behind her. In deference to the heat, she'd pulled her hair up and Jase took advantage of it, gently kissing the nape of her neck. A shiver coursed over her skin, and hard as she tried to resist, it reminded her of the day she'd arrived—how desire had flared so quickly between them it had taken her breath away. She should have run then, when she'd had the chance.

She ought to run now.

Almost as if he'd read her mind, Jase curled an arm around her waist. He moved close, until his chest hit her shoulder blades, and rested his cheek just above her ear. They stood there like that, swaying slightly, with only the rustle of horse hooves on hay to disturb the quiet. Rae expected to feel hemmed in, but peace filled her instead.

She knew it was dangerous to relax, but it felt so good to lean against Jase. Like coming home.

Jason Van Allen was as rock solid a man as God had ever made, in every way. And tall and handsome, with sun-bleached hair, sparkling brown eyes and a smile that lit up his whole face. He made her knees go weak. And her heart soften.

More importantly to Rae, Jase could be depended on. He would never intentionally hurt her, and she knew he'd be there if she needed him, in good times and bad. He'd all but come right out and said he wanted the chance to prove it.

To a man like Jase, that would mean marriage.

That idea crept in through the chinks in her armored heart, though she tried to stop it. She could almost, *almost,* see a future for herself with Jase. She closed her eyes, knowing she'd never be able to forget the way it felt to have his arms around her like this, to feel such absolute contentment—

Something wet slid down the side of her cheek, and Rae jerked away. Her eyes flew open, nearly crossing in an effort to focus on the soft brown muzzle of the bay mare only inches from her own nose.

Jase's body shook against hers as he chuckled. She felt his warm breath against her ear and an almost physical jolt as the joyful sound of his laughter wrapped around her heart.

"My sister Jo used to spoil the horses with carrots and apples," he said, his voice deep and soft in her ear. "Goldie here must have smelled your perfume and thought she was in for a snack."

Rae didn't answer, so Jase took the opportunity to drag her a little more into his world. "Jo has the softest heart of anyone I've ever met. She was forever taking care of something or someone. She'd be glad to know I'm not lonely while my parents are away, and that you're taking such good care of me."

Rae stiffened and started to ease away. Jase let her go as if he'd intended to all along, curling his arm around her shoulders and steering her away from the horse stall. "Jo got married not too long ago. But you know that.

"My brother Jon is a chef in New York, which is pretty amazing considering the fact that he never stepped into a kitchen until Jo started learning to cook. She needed a guinea pig to test her recipes on. Jon could never refuse her anything, so he learned to cook right along with her, out of self-defense."

They walked out of the barn and Jase led Rae toward the farm's office. She didn't acknowledge his sudden nostalgic bent—or object to it—so he kept talking. "My other brother, Jacob, became a lawyer in New York, which didn't surprise anyone because he argues about everything." He laughed, forgetting that he was reminiscing for Rae's sake and not his own. "Jake could convince you it was midnight at high noon. He says he's going to be the Chief Justice of the Supreme Court one day and I believe him."

"And what about you?" Rae asked quietly. "Your sister is an author and your brothers are both well on their way to making their own marks in the world. Don't you want to do the same?"

"I'm happy right where I am. This farm has been in my family for two hundred years—"

Rae shrugged his arm off, and Jase realized he'd hit a sore spot. Her father had thrown that in her face too often for her not to be touchy about it, but he refused to cater to her sensitivity. It was time she got over the past.

Before she could put more space between them, Jase caught her hand, twining his fingers with hers. She seemed to calm with his touch, and he couldn't stifle a slight smile, knowing he had that effect on her.

"Jon, Jake and I grew up here together. We used to fight, and complain about our annoying little sister always tagging along behind us. Mom and Dad were strict when it came to discipline, but love and security were things we took for granted. We had the best kind of childhood you could imagine, but that didn't stop Jake and Jon and Jo from leaving, and it's not what holds me here."

"I get the feeling there's a moral to your story," she said dryly.

"And I'm willing to bet you know what it is."

Rae sighed. Of course she knew what he was getting at. She shouldn't let her past dictate her future. But Jase had no idea that the ideal childhood he'd described only made hers look more pitiful. There had been no laughter in her home, no brother or sister to fight and play and commiserate with. No discipline had been necessary because she'd been too cowed to get into trouble, felt too worthless to make friends, even if her father would have allowed her any kind of social life.

She'd escaped that dark, lonely, depressing place and she cherished her freedom. It wasn't something she'd give up easily. Rae wished she could make Jase understand how she felt, but there were no words—at least none that wouldn't hurt him.

He, too, seemed content to let the matter alone for the time being.

Jase opened the door to the row house at the opposite end from the one Rae was using, and she knew almost before she stepped inside that it was his private domain. It smelled like Jase—spice and hardworking man, with just a hint of cigar smoke. The small front room was paneled with golden knotty pine, and an antique rolltop desk holding a state-of-the-art computer and printer looked ready for business. A burgundy leather sofa and chair flanked a small coffee table, and the kitchenette was outfitted with a bar and tall stools.

What really caught Rae's attention, though, was the painting hanging over the sofa. It fit the room's decor with its slashing bands of burgundy and gold amid blendings of darker color, but it was the power of the piece that drew Rae to it. She found herself standing in front of the abstract vision with no memory of crossing the threshold or the room. All she saw was an artistic composition full of emotion, anger and loneliness boldly and movingly expressed, fear and frustration lurking in the shadows. A serene shade of cerulean blue seemed to promise hope, but it was easy to overlook amidst the wild swirl of oils.

"Chase painted that."

Rae started at the sound of Jase's voice close beside her. "It reminds me of some of the photographs I took when I first picked up a camera," she said, more to herself than Jase. Her earliest images had been dark and disturbing, even to those who didn't understand the artistic facet of photography.

"You know, in all the time you've been here, I've never seen your work," Jase said. "I'd like to sometime."

"Uh, sure," Rae replied hesitantly. But she knew she'd find a way to avoid that. Even though she'd long since exorcised the troubled part of her soul from her work, it was too much like baring herself to him, in a way almost more personal than taking off her clothes.

Jase already knew her too well to let him see inside her soul.

It disturbed her even more that he seemed to realize that her feelings about her work were too sensitive to explore. He didn't like encountering something he couldn't knock down or go around or climb over; Rae could see that.

"Can you ride a horse?" he asked, and the suddenness of his bright smile after that somber moment disarmed her completely.

She smiled tentatively in response and nodded, knowing that even if she'd never sat a horse before in her life, she'd have agreed to anything to keep that smile on his face.

She tried not to dwell on why his happiness was so important to her.

Rae let Goldie—the same bay mare she'd admired earlier—have her head, confident she would follow along behind her stable mate. That left *her* free to admire the way Jase sat so tall and easy on his mount. He could have been a part of the graceful horseflesh underneath him, his big body shifting effortlessly with the animal's movements.

She would have been helplessly mired in desire, too, if she wasn't in mortal agony. They'd only been in the saddle for about an hour, but it felt like forever to the inside of her thighs. Aside from her backside being numb, the rest of her wasn't too bad off, but she had a feeling it was all going to catch up with her before long.

Aside from Jase, there was little to take her mind off her discomfort—the scenery certainly didn't. In fact, her current surroundings only added insult to injury.

They'd been climbing steadily through woods so thick there were places they barely squeezed between the tree trunks. A heavy undergrowth of ferns brushed the bottoms of her stirrups. Each step the mare took stirred up a cloud of mosquitoes, which the shade and still air under the heavy canopy of leaves did nothing to dispel. The industrial-strength insect repellent Jase had insisted she use helped a little. At least the number of bites had stayed in the single digits.

Rae had just begun to wonder what could be worth this jungle trek when sunlight burst through the tree-tops overhead. She craned her neck to look over Jase's shoulder, then nudged her mount with her heels so it would move up beside his.

Jase reined up in a meadow about two acres square, filled with waist-high grasses and wildflowers. He swung one long, muscular leg over his horse with a limber grace that Rae envied. When she got a look at the vista spread out before her, though, she stopped wondering if her thighs would ever get to know each other again.

Their hilltop seemed to be the highest land around for miles. More hills rippled away into the distance, some crowned with similar small meadows, others wearing a mantle of deep green pine forest dappled with the lighter greens of birch, oak and aspen. The sky was filled with puffy white clouds, and land and sky seemed to merge at the curved horizon.

The most beautiful sight by far was the deep blue lake nestled in the valley directly below. A slight breeze stirred the treetops of the forest, making it look like a restless green ocean. But the surface of the lake remained mirror flat, almost magically calm.

Rae eased off her horse and walked slowly to the brink of the hill, not realizing Jase was beside her until he spoke.

"Breathtaking, isn't it?"

"It's like a different world," she said. And much to her surprise, she found that she didn't want to photograph it.

She had no doubt she could capture the absolute serenity of the place, but there was something so . . . elemental about the lake and the hills around it, something so precious and private. She could tell by looking at Jase's face that it was a very special place for him. That he'd chosen to share it with her meant a great deal.

It felt so right, so perfect just to stand there and let the tranquillity of the place seep into her heart and soul. She took a deep breath, savoring the fresh air. The sunshine wrapped around her, warm as a mother's hug, and the breeze caressed her skin and stirred her hair ever so slightly.

It was by no means silent in that beautiful meadow. The birds sang and the long grass rustled, but Rae almost resented Jase when he disturbed the moment. Almost.

"I've always thought this was about as close to heaven as I could get," Jase said, his deep voice hushed.

Rae looked up into his face, surprised to find the same reverence there that she felt. "It's wonderful, Jase. I've never seen anyplace so beautiful."

He turned to her, his brown eyes piercing, boring into hers. "But you will eventually, Rae. You want to travel the world and photograph it. You'll see hundreds of places at least this beautiful, and before long you'll forget all about this little piece of Wisconsin forest."

Rae opened her mouth to deny it, but she couldn't. Not because Jase was right, but because she didn't want to admit that this peaceful landscape would forever be entwined with her memories of Jase Van Allen. It would be easier, she knew, to think of him here rather than surrounded by farm buildings. Seeing Jase like this, with his face raised to the sun and framed by nature, made it harder to justify her decision to leave.

Fourteen

She'd gone, left him without even saying good-bye.

When Jase couldn't find Rae, it was his first thought, because it was his worst fear.

Teeth clenched so tight his jaw ached, he stood inside the barn where he'd last seen her. No matter what the emergency, no matter that she'd insisted on moving that family of newborn kittens to a clean stall, he shouldn't have left her alone there.

On Norge Farm, that barn was little more than a huge signpost, something big enough to both identify and advertise the place. But its stereotypical architecture and faded red and white paint job had undoubtedly reminded Rae of her unhappy childhood. Even if Jase hadn't assumed there was one like it where she'd grown up, he'd have had to be blind to miss the apprehension in her eyes when she had walked in.

The memory of it still tore at him, more deeply because he had such wonderful memories of the old building.

Jase knew, though, that Rae had never lain up in the prickly hay loft, breathing the air, counting the stripes of sky visible between the century-old boards, and daydreaming. She'd never jumped from that loft and known what it was like to fly, if only for a split second before the mounds of hay rushed up to meet her.

The risk of injury had only made the experience more exhilarating, but Jase had a feeling that, aside from leaving home, Rae had never taken a risk in her life. Oh, her profession was chancy in its way, but it didn't challenge her to change inside. She hid behind her ambition, used it as an excuse to avoid her feelings. Especially her feelings for him.

Only the piteous mewing of helpless kittens could have convinced her to enter the barn, which had to be a potent symbol of her past. It certainly hadn't been her desire to be with him.

Even as that resentful thought crossed his mind, Jase knew he wasn't being fair. Rae had really been trying the last couple of days—ever since their afternoon on that magical hilltop.

He'd taken her there hoping she would see that there was incredible peace and beauty at Norge Farm, not just reminders of the ugliness she'd been raised in. It had seemed to work, too.

For the last two days they'd been together, night and day. Jase knew it hadn't always been easy for Rae, but he was proud of her for facing down her fears, and touched that she was doing it for him.

Even if she wouldn't admit she cared.

Jase took one last look at the cat family, now resettled in a new stall, as clean and neat a job as he'd have done himself. But then, Rae took her work very seriously. He admired that about her. And hated it.

Jase stepped out into the achingly bright sunlight, but all he could see were Rae's eyes. In silence she'd watched him walk away, and when he'd glanced back at her, her beautiful blue eyes had been clouded. She'd been chewing on the inside of her cheek like she did when she was nervous. And when she was nervous or unsure, there was only one thing that would calm her.

She hadn't touched a camera in days. The fact that she'd retreated into her work just now stung.

It wasn't reasonable to be jealous of a thing. And Jase knew that if Rae were ever to be a permanent part of his life, he'd have to learn to live with her sometimes fanatical preoccupation with photography. It would be a hell of a lot easier, he thought grimly, if he knew she loved him.

The front door of the row house was open. Jase nearly ripped the screen door off in his eagerness to find Rae. A quick but thorough search of the ground floor didn't turn her up, so he took the stairs two at a time, heading for the little loft bedroom she had turned into a darkroom. A *temporary* darkroom, he reminded himself, as he stopped on the narrow landing at the top of the stairs. As temporary a fixture in her life as she intended him to be.

He stopped cold at the closed door, though it was less daunting than the invisible ones Rae kept closing between them. Deciding to force the issue of her feelings was one thing, going through with it wasn't nearly as easy.

Taking a deep breath, he eased the door open just a crack in case she was developing, he told himself. But when he saw that the light was on, he ran out of excuses.

Jase nudged the door wider, and a wave of heat hit him, not due entirely to the stifling air in the totally closed room. Rae stood near the far wall with her back to him, so intent on something she held in her hand that she didn't even know she wasn't alone anymore.

Jase took the opportunity to indulge himself.

Rae had put her hair up in an untidy knot, undoubtedly to ease her work rather than help her keep cool. Bits of hay clung to her deep auburn hair, and her T-shirt was damp between her shoulder blades. The satiny bare skin of her neck, arms and legs glistened as it had in the sauna.

Remembrance streaked through his brain and heat sizzled along his nerve endings. He could still taste the musk of her skin as his lips caressed the long, elegant line of her back, still feel the resilient softness of her waist in his hands, her supple strength as she moved over and around him.

His lower body clenched with rock-hard need. An almost desperate yearning rose within him, clouding his mind when she half turned toward him. But she still didn't seem to see anything besides the photo she held in her hands.

She ran her fingertips almost reverently over the glossy eight-by-ten print, her gaze focused raptly on whatever image she'd captured. It was the touch of a lover, Jase realized, and his jealousy flared to life again. Not over the subject in the picture, but the process of creating it.

"You got the kittens nicely set up," he said, his voice harsh with desire and jealousy.

Her head snapped around at the same instant she slapped the photo facedown on the table beside her. Then she turned her body and slid a half step to stand directly in front of it. Curiosity didn't entirely douse his lust, but at least it gave Jase something else to concentrate on.

He took a step into the room, smiling almost wolfishly when she backed up in automatic reaction.

"I'd have cleaned the stall later," he said, gradually bringing his voice down to a soothing level. "You could have come with me—"

"Why?" she demanded, the confusion in her eyes clearing into understanding. And anger. "Because you didn't want to leave me alone in that old barn?"

"Yes." He held her gaze, his eyes intent and unapologetic as he took another step into the room.

Rae closed her eyes because she couldn't keep looking at him and hang on to her fraying self-control at the same time. It had been one hell of a day, and judging by the look on Jase's face, he wasn't going to let it fade slowly into the peace of twilight. And maybe that was for the best.

She had nearly gotten her aversion to farms under control—until she and Jase had stepped into that hulking structure—a reminder of all the worst times in her life. She had stayed there after he'd been called away, foolishly trying to prove she'd gotten over the past. She'd only proven that all the determination in the world didn't count for much when her memories kicked in.

Knowing Jase was watching her—watching and waiting—didn't help. "I didn't tell you about my past so you'd treat me like glass." But she was thinking about what had happened after he'd left her alone.

Trying desperately to control her panic, she had dragged the bale of fresh straw Jase had left her and began to spread it in the cleaned stall. In seconds her deliberately calm movements had grown frantic, until she was throwing straw so fast the air was filled with it.

She didn't even remember transferring the kittens to their new clean home, although the long scratch on her left arm had to be from their nervous mother. The first memory Rae had was of finding herself in the darkroom, chest heaving, until the smell of the developing solution had brought her a measure of comfort—and finally some peace.

Hard-won peace.

She didn't want questions now, didn't want anything to deter her from getting back to the reality she'd buried over the past few days. She needed her camera, and the work that would remind her who she was, what she wanted to be and where she belonged.

Jase needed to understand that, though it wouldn't be easy to tell him.

Rae opened her eyes and found him only inches

from her, and choked on the words. She retreated, far enough to find her voice—and her determination.

"I told you about my childhood so you would understand why I can't stay here much longer, Jase."

"Then what's been going on the last two days?" he demanded harshly. "Hell, Rae, you've been my shadow during the day and a damn sight closer than that at night. Are you trying to drive me crazy? Showing me what we could have right before you rip it away?"

"You asked me to spend time with you—" Rae broke off, refusing to let him put her on the defensive.

"And that's all it takes? Any guy who asks you to spend time with him gets this kind of one on one?" Jase knew it wasn't fair to use the sex they'd shared as a weapon against her, but she'd left him no choice. He had to get through to her, whatever it took.

"Of course not," she hissed. "You know I was attracted to you the moment we met."

"You've already admitted as much."

"Well, then," she said, as if that explained everything.

Jase exhaled in one long, frustrated breath. He wasn't getting anywhere this way. There had to be another key . . .

His gaze fell to the photo she'd been studying when he found her. Out of the corner of his eye he saw her lunge for it, so he scooped it up first.

But he looked at her instead of it. "I probably wouldn't have thought twice about this if you hadn't panicked."

"I didn't panic," she said heatedly.

"That's how it looked to me." Jase glanced absently at the photo, up into her flushed face again. Then he looked back down.

Slowly he held up the photograph, allowing himself a wide smile—identical to the one he wore in the picture. "I hate to sound vain, Rae, but you certainly did me justice."

A sound issued from the back of her throat, something between the growl of an enraged lioness and absolute humiliation. "I took that the day I was in town waiting for Kurt. I thought you were him."

Jase ducked under the drying line and looked at the other pictures hanging there. "Maybe the first one, but a whole roll?"

Rae knew what he was seeing, and her face grew so hot the tips of her ears felt like they'd caught fire. Every single photo was Jase, with that same incredible smile that had illuminated his face the moment he'd turned and caught sight of her.

It was a far cry from the self-congratulatory, purely macho grin splitting his handsome face at the moment. "You surprised me," she grumbled. Her voice didn't sound very convincing to her own ears, but she could hardly tell him that his smile had so amazed her. That she could bring him such joy touched her in places she hadn't even known existed. She'd just had to capture it.

But if Jase was smug now, she could just imagine what would happen if she admitted all that. "I just froze with my finger on the automatic shutter."

He chuckled and moved toward her. "I don't believe you."

Rae stepped back. If he touched her, she would be lost.

Hoping she'd managed to make her expression uncaring, she shrugged. "It happened so fast. It must have been one of those moments when everything comes together. A good subject, the right light . . . I didn't even remember what was on this roll until I developed it."

"Then you weren't caressing that photo because it was me, you were just pleased with your work."

Rae shrugged again, and stared at him coolly, though it was the hardest thing she'd ever done.

Jase ran a hand through his hair and laughed again. But this time the sound was a little more uncertain. She should have been happy that she'd managed to convince him, at least partly, that the photos meant nothing, but knowing she had hurt him in the process made her feel lower than a snake in the grass.

He stalked to within a foot of her and reached out. Rae flinched, but he closed his fingers an inch short of her chin, then dropped his hand. "You're going to keep denying you feel anything for me but lust."

She jolted at that term.

His smile turned almost feral and he seemed to loom over her, sensing her weakness like a true predator. "You're the one who claims that's all we have between us. You phrased it more nicely, but that's what it boils down to."

"You have no idea what I'm feeling."

The lines of strain disappeared from between his brows, and he leaned against the table, visibly relaxed. "Don't ever play poker, Rae. Or if you do, don't bluff."

She felt her face heat again and told herself it was anger this time. "I may not be able to hide my feelings, but you don't have any qualms at taking advantage of them."

"All's fair in love and war. You've heard the phrase,

haven't you?" His face went from teasing to intense in the split second between breaths.

Rae backed up until her shoulder blades hit the wall. It wasn't far enough. "I love you, Rae," Jase rasped. "And here's something else you're not ready to hear. I want to marry you. You can run away, but it won't change the way I feel about you."

She could only stare. Even when he shook his head and let his shoulders slump, she couldn't bring herself to answer him. Rae didn't know what to say, what to feel about his declaration, but it should have been simple to answer his proposal. A week ago it would have been the most natural thing in the world to say no.

Now, all she could do was stand there, her eyes dry and aching, her throat burning as if she'd guzzled the developing solution.

His eyes went from hopeful to hard. He shoved his hands into his pockets and turned away. "You know where I am," he said over his shoulder, and walked out the door.

And she let him go.

Fifteen

Rae sank to the floor and wrapped her arms around her knees, hugging them tight against her chest. It didn't relieve the ache, any more than her surroundings did. Images of Jase were everywhere, not only hanging from the drying line, but inside of her, where she couldn't take them down and hide them. He filled her thoughts and every shadowy corner of her heart.

Jase had given her all of himself, unselfishly, and she had used him up. She had taken a man who exuded contentment and vitality and made him sad and gloomy. And he'd done nothing to deserve it.

She'd never come to terms with her past, but was that his fault? Her bitterness and resentment had actually seemed normal—until Jase came along to show her what it was like to live in the light and warmth of love. His love.

He'd welcomed her with open arms and open heart, and all she had done was push him away without giving anything in return. No matter what had happened to her, it was over now. And there was no excuse for treating any human being like that, especially someone who cared so deeply for her.

He deserved something from her—at the very least an apology. And the truth.

Hard as she searched within herself, Rae had no idea what the truth was, but she got to her feet anyway. She didn't like uncertainty; she'd always made absolutely sure she knew just what she wanted and where she was headed before she made any move. Until now.

It wasn't easy for her to walk out that door and look for Jase while her mind was running in confused circles, but she did it. By the time she found him in his office, she felt lightheaded and sick to her stomach. It was dizzying, not knowing what she was going to do or say.

In a strange way, though, it was also liberating. It felt good to go with the sweeter emotion of the present instead of letting the darkness of her past guide her.

Jase didn't look up when she entered, but Rae saw the muscles in his jaw tighten, and her heart ached. Only days before he'd greeted her with a smile so bright it lit up her entire life. Now she inspired anger in him, and she saw wariness in his rich brown eyes when he finally looked over at her.

Her throat clogged with emotion, and she had to blink against the tears gathering in her eyes. "I . . think we should talk."

Jase only stared, as if he could see right into her soul.

Rae twined her fingers together to keep them from shaking. "But if you're busy . . ." Her voice trailed off suggestively, but his expression never changed, neither inviting her to continue or declining her company.

"You're not going to make this easy on me, are you?"

"All you have to do is turn around and walk out the door."

Anger blazed to life inside her, anger and frustration. "If it was so easy for me to turn my back, knowing I had hurt you, do you think I'd be standing here now?"

A slight smile curved his chiseled mouth, a mere ghost of the joy he had once found in her presence. But a little of the darkness inside her retreated.

"I have no idea where to begin," she said, then paused to work the quaver out of her voice—and because she truly had no idea what to say.

Jase didn't feel the need to fill the silence, and the fact that he was watching her so intently only made it more difficult to think. She couldn't look into his expectant eyes, not knowing what might come out of her mouth. It would be the truth, but would that truth hurt him more than she already had?

Rae's eyes wandered to the painting she had so loved the first time she'd come into Jase's office. It struck her anew how much that painting called to her, with its expressive slashes of vivid color. She could have created it out of her own inner turmoil—if she hadn't had her own medium.

Instead of oils, she channeled all her feelings into her photography, portraying her sorrow or her joy, whatever she was feeling at the moment. But she'd been denied that over the last few days, and the photos she'd developed of Jase had hardly helped her sort out her feelings.

For the first time since she picked up a camera, she began to see that her art was also her obsession, and that it had a destructive side. She *had* used it to shield herself from life, never daring to admit how emotionally distant she really was.

Rae looked at that painting and understood exactly what Jase's brother-in-law had been feeling when he had painted it. She felt the pain and uncertainty in every brush stroke, all the pent-up yearning and frustration of someone locked within himself, who wouldn't reach out for the good in life because he'd been burned too many times.

She looked back at Jase and summed up their entire relationship in two words. "I'm afraid."

He closed his eyes and dropped his head back, exhaling heavily in relief.

"Of you," she added, hating the words, hating how his head snapped up and his gaze whipped to hers. He unfolded his long body and crossed the room in two strides, grasping her upper arms in his large, strong hands and lifting her to her toes.

"When are you going to figure out that I'm not like your father?" he rasped in a voice thick with leashed violence. "All this time you've been saying it's the farm you can't stomach, but the real truth is that you're afraid I'll turn into an ogre like him and make your life hell someday."

Rae wanted to deny it, but she couldn't. "I know it never made any sense, Jase," she whispered.

He let go of her as if she'd burned him. "It makes perfect sense." He ran a hand through his sun-bleached hair. "You wouldn't be so scared unless you were in love with me."

Jase expected her to deny it, but she straightened, lifting her chin. The defiance on her face would have made him smile if the situation wasn't so serious. The rest of his life hung in the balance; he couldn't afford to make any mistakes now.

"You asked me to marry you," she said with quiet dignity. "But if I said yes and tried to live here with you, I'd only make you miserable. Maybe not now, maybe not next year, but eventually you'll start to resent the time I have to spend on the road, and the countless hours I'll have to spend in the darkroom."

"No, but—"

"Besides, you want children, Jase. I know we've never discussed it, but any fool could see you'd be an incredible father."

"And you'd be an incredible mother, Rae." He reached out and laid his hand over her flat belly.

He saw her eyes soften for just a second before apprehension closed in again and she backed away from his touch. "I never gave it much thought."

"Until lately."

Rae's breath caught, and realization flooded her, but she couldn't allow herself to be sidetracked, even by the wonderful idea of carrying Jase's child. "No matter what else I might do in my life, photography will always be a very important part of it. I've worked hard to get this far. I can't afford to stop pushing now when I'm not even close to meeting my goals."

She held up a hand when he started to comment. "Don't think I'm still using my career as an excuse. I'm not, but I won't give it up, even though I love you, Jase, but if things work out the way I want them to, I won't have the kind of job that—"

Jase reached out and tilted her face to his. "What did you say? Say it again!"

She brushed his hand off her chin. "Say what?"

"What you just said." Jase sighed. "You were talking about your career."

Rae frowned in puzzlement. "I can't give it up, Jase."

"Even though . . ." he prompted.

"Even though . . . I love you."

Jase wrapped his arms around her and pulled her into an embrace. Had he lifted her up? Rae suddenly felt a sensation of lightness, as if the weight of the world had just lifted off her. Or maybe it was the weight of her past.

For the first time in her entire life, she felt free.

She threw her arms around Jase's neck and held on to him with every ounce of strength she possessed. "I love you," she murmured breathlessly against his throat. "But—"

"Then we can work all the rest of it out." Jase pressed his mouth to her temple. He'd heard the wonder in her voice, but there had been fear there, too. "There's nothing for you to be afraid of, Rae. I would never knowingly do anything to hurt you. I promise."

Rae leaned back and took his face in her hands, studying his eyes. She saw sincerity there, and so much love that her own eyes blurred. "What if I hurt you, Jase?"

"That's a risk I'm willing to take."

"But—"

He silenced her with a passionate kiss, groaning when she melted into him. In seconds the fire raged between them, hotter and fiercer than ever before.

She loved him; he'd give her time to get used to that. Commitment would come later.

Rae didn't know how they got to the couch, but somewhere in the frenzy to make love once more she was able to think for a second or two.

Jase loved her so unselfishly. She could return his love, at least, even if she couldn't give him everything he wanted. And as long as they were together, she could give him all of herself.

Gently she pulled away from him and stood by the couch, smiling at his passion-dazed frown. He reached for her, but she fended him off. Very slowly, allowing nothing but his gaze to touch her, she undressed herself, and then started on his clothing.

"No, let me," she said when he tried to help.

"You're killing me," he ground out through clenched teeth. But he kept his hands at his sides, moving only when she needed to pull his shirt out from under him, then his faded blue jeans and soft cotton briefs.

Rae had always let Jase set the tone and pace of their lovemaking, meeting him as eagerly or as leisurely as he wanted. Now she took the lead.

She sat on the edge of the couch and ran her hands slowly over his body. The muscles rippled under his hot skin, quivering at her touch, and she trembled deep inside. The pleasure she gave him only intensified her own.

She could see the pulse beating strongly in Jase's throat. His breath grew ragged, as ragged as hers when she worked her way back up from his feet, kneading her fingers into the muscles of his calves and thighs, then ran them into the thatch of dark, springy hair at his groin.

Her hand closed around his rigid manhood, and his body jackknifed. A groan tore from so deep within him Rae swore she felt it vibrate through her. Or maybe that was her own moan of need.

Jase threaded his fingers into the hair at her nape, his callused thumbs rubbing over her cheeks and lips. Rae bit delicately into the pad of his thumb and saw the fire in his eyes rage higher before he dropped his mouth to hers.

She lost control momentarily as her fingers convulsed around him, her other hand dug into his biceps and she matched his wildness. She pulled back in one last attempt to tame the need erupting within her.

Jase had only to move his lips to her neck and she surrendered again. She didn't protest when he laid her back, didn't feel the cool leather against her heated skin because her senses were full of the man she loved.

He drew one aching nipple into his mouth and she cried out at the exquisite torture, her voice desperate with need.

"Say it, Rae," he rasped.

She writhed as his hot breath teased her ear. "What?" she groaned helplessly.

"Tell me how you feel."

Her heart skipped a beat. She could no more ignore his plea than she could the demands he'd ignited in her body. "I love you," she whispered, fighting to see him through a sheen of tears.

His handsome face relaxed into an expression of such joy she couldn't stop her tears from spilling over.

"Hey, what's this?" He smoothed his fingers over her wet cheeks.

Rae took a deep, shuddering breath. "I love you, Jase. And I'll always love you, no matter what," she said fiercely.

He gathered her to him and held her close, just held her as if it were the last time. She'd never had love in her life, he reassured himself. Once she trusted him not to hurt her, she wouldn't want to leave.

She twisted against him, one sinuous head to toe caress of soft, supple flesh that drove everything else from his mind. Jase eased back against the couch, pulling her down with him so that they lay on their sides, face to face.

Rae didn't need any urging to keep her gaze on his. Though she felt more naked than she ever had, she let him see all the love she had to give and all the pleasure he gave her.

Jase took her back to paradise, but slowly this time, with soft caresses and gentle, deep kisses. He pulled her thigh up over his side and slipped into her sweetness, stroking long and slow, maddeningly slow, yet the end came much too soon.

Rae moaned, low and deep as ecstasy poured through her like a river of molten gold, warm and precious, slow but exquisitely unstoppable. She came apart in Jase's arms, and felt him cradle and protect her even as he joined her in that long, shuddering wave of motion and emotion.

Her body tingled, replete, but not as satisfied as her heart. "I love you, Jase," she breathed, right before she drifted off in his arms.

It must still be so new to her, Jase supposed, yet each time Rae spoke her feelings it seemed easier for her. He pulled her close, cradling her head on his shoulder and fighting the urge to shake her out of her sated slumber and make her say she loved him again.

God willing, he'd be hearing it for the rest of his life.

Sixteen

Rae should have felt self-conscious walking around Jase's kitchen wearing nothing but a nearly transparent cotton nightie, but she delighted in the way his eyes warmed every time he looked at her, the way his hand crept out to touch her bare skin—as often as she found herself needing to touch him. Only hours ago it would have felt too much like she was making herself at home. Like she was *making* a home. Now she didn't care. The truth had done that for her, made her feel free and confident. Facing her fear—her real fear—seemed to have taken away its power to control her.

And she loved Jase even more for forcing her to do it. She knew she'd never be able to repay him, but she wanted to try. Even if it took a lifetime.

He pulled her down onto his lap, tracing her cheekbones, the bridge of her nose and her eyebrows with one gentle fingertip. "I can't remember what my life was like before you showed up on my doorstep, Raelynn Morgan."

"You didn't seem to be suffering," she teased, but Rae felt her smile tremble, partly from emotion, partly from remembrance of the very first time she'd seen him.

Desire had struck her so fast and hard when she'd seen him standing at the pump that day, bare-chested and dripping. His irreverent grin had dazzled her, drawn her into a dizzying whirlwind of a ride that she wouldn't have traded for all the money and fame in the world.

When she looked past the contentment of the moment, though, she saw the shadows that she had put in Jase's eyes, and it tore at her, because she couldn't give him the promises he needed.

It was just too soon, she told herself. But, as Jase's voice drew her back to the wonderful coziness of his kitchen, a part of her feared it would always be too soon.

"I was happy enough, Rae. I've had a pretty good life so far, but you brought something into it that I didn't even realize I was missing."

He looked like he was going to say something else, then thought better of it. Rae didn't push. Much as she wished otherwise, she had fears of her own that made her leery of opening doors that were better left shut.

Instead she dropped her mouth to his, letting her actions say what she couldn't put into words. There was desire in the kiss, but she poured her heart and soul into it, too.

Jase seemed to understand. He met her almost reverently, his hands cruising gently over her as his mouth worshipped hers.

Rae kissed him harder, aroused once more. When Jase tore free, she threaded her fingers into the hair at the nape of his neck and tugged, hard.

"Ouch!" Jase exclaimed, but quietly as he pulled her hands from around his neck. "I thought I heard something."

He turned toward the door, listening intently. Just as he was about to admit he must have been mistaken, a distinctly automotive thud sounded from the drive in front of the house.

"Was that a car door?"

He nodded, then grabbed her when she tried to slip off his lap.

She tried to peel his hands off her waist, but he held on tight. "It might be your parents."

"It can't be my parents. I told them not to come back yet."

Rae whipped around to look at him, her mouth open and a hot tide of red climbing her cheeks. "Then I guess it doesn't matter if they catch me half-naked in your lap. I'm sure they've already figured out what's going on between us."

"They knew before we did," Jase pointed out. "Why do you think they left us alone?"

Her face grew so heated he was afraid she'd spontaneously ignite. Then again, from the look in her eyes, she might not be the one in physical danger.

"It's just one of the men coming in from town," he soothed, rubbing his hands up and down her back.

Jase felt some of the tension drain out of her, but she didn't fully relax, not the way she had this afternoon when she had finally admitted she loved him. The memory still filled him with something like awe.

She loved him.

Not enough, though, he thought, resting his cheek

on the upper slope of her breast and pulling her close. He wished he could reach into her mind and somehow erase all the old, hurtful memories, all the pain and fear and anger she'd lived with her whole life.

But he couldn't. That was a battle Rae had to fight on her own. Somewhere inside herself she had to find the strength to put the past behind her. The most he could do was give her the room to do it—and be there for her if she needed him.

And maybe nudging her a bit wouldn't hurt.

"When's the last time you talked to your father, Rae?"

Rae sucked in a breath, the sound harsh in the sudden silence. She slammed her palms into his shoulders and shoved with all her might. Jase held on to her until she gave up. Her back was stiff and she refused to look at him, though, and he knew if he let go she'd be out of the room like a shot.

"When's the last time you went home?"

If possible, Rae stiffened even further. "My home is in Chicago."

"You know what I mean."

The resistance drained out of her, but her eyes were cold. "Every year on my father's birthday, I call him. The conversations last all of about thirty seconds, and I do all the talking. He's always too busy for me to come there, and he always has a reason why he can't come to Chicago. Running a farm is a lot of work when you don't have a son to help you."

Jase cursed, long and low. He'd never met Ray Morgan, yet there seemed to be plenty of reasons to hate the man. By avoiding her attempts at reconciliation, her father made it that much harder for her to heal.

Yet Rae still loved the man. Her boundless capacity

for love was heartening. Despite everything her father had done and was still doing, Rae hadn't become sour and bitter.

Jase kissed her, a gesture filled with everything he felt for her. Love and desire, respect and compassion. And determination. Come hell or high water, he'd find a way to keep her here. He knew that in time he could help her put her painful memories behind her and face the future, with all the promise it held for them. And, in time, he'd give her a family of her own. When she was ready.

She sighed softly, and Jase felt the tension slowly drain from her as she lost herself in a kiss that gradually turned more carnal. He knew she was letting the fire of passion burn away the unhappiness, but he was content to be used this one time.

He slipped his hand up to her breast, and Rae murmured with pleasure once more.

"Well, isn't this a cozy scene."

They both froze for a few precious seconds before Rae tore herself out of Jase's arms and raced to the coat rack. She pulled on one of his old flannel shirts, clutching it together over her breasts as she turned to face the door.

Jase swallowed a curse, watching her shock fade to relief as she ran across the kitchen and hugged Chrissy.

"I hate to barge in like this," Chrissy said, "but I knocked and you two didn't hear me. If I had known why—"

Rae made a distressed noise that stopped Chrissy mid-sentence. It didn't sit well with Jase. He hated knowing she was embarrassed at being caught in his arms. If it had been his parents, he'd have understood, but Chrissy was her best friend—almost like a

sister, Rae had said. She should have wanted to share
her new feelings with someone so close to her.

Unless she didn't intend to stay.

"I should be furious at you for taking off like that,"
Rae said, hugging her friend again. "But I'm so
happy to see you."

Chrissy raised one perfectly plucked eyebrow in his
direction. "I don't think Jase is."

He didn't bother to deny it. "Well, we weren't exactly expecting you."

Chrissy sighed, and Jase swore he saw an apologetic
look flash across her beautiful face before she turned
to Rae. "I was dying to find out what happened between you two . . . and it's nice to know I was right
for a change." She grinned at the way Rae blushed
when she glanced at Jase.

"That's not the real reason you're here," he
growled.

"No." Chrissy's hundred-watt smile dimmed. She
pulled an envelope out of her purse and handed it
to Rae.

And the world seemed to jerk to a halt for Jase. He
didn't need to know what was in that envelope to
figure out the moment he'd been dreading had arrived. The moment Rae would have to make up her
mind whether to stay or go.

Judging from the bleak expression on Rae's face
when she looked at him, she knew it, too.

But it was worse than he could possibly have
guessed.

Rae tore the envelope open and pulled out a single
sheet of heavy stationery, the slight tremor in her
hand growing until she could hardly read the boldly
scrawled words. "It's from Morris."

"My father," Chrissy supplied helpfully, then

snapped her mouth shut when Jase shot her a look hot enough to scorch an iceberg.

Rae sank down in the nearest chair, her face white and her breathing labored. "*Epoch* found out about what's happening up here and they want to do a piece on it," she said in a hushed voice. "They want me."

"What is *Epoch*?"

"A very trendy new magazine, ultra popular with the twenty-five to forty crowd," Chrissy supplied, although Jase noticed she made a point of not looking at him. "If she does it well, an assignment like this could put Rae on top. Every magazine editor in the country will be offering her work."

"They want an article, too," Rae said in a weak, wavery voice.

Chrissy's mouth dropped open. "Daddy didn't tell me that!" she squealed. She launched herself at Rae, tearing the note out of her hand and reading it herself. "Do you realize what this could mean?"

Rae slumped into a chair. "I'm not sure I can write anything more than a caption or two, and they want a whole article."

Chrissy made a derisive sound. "Of course you can, and you'll ace that, too. My father wouldn't have told you about this if he didn't think you were capable, and we both know he's always right. Haven't all of his protégés proven that?"

Jase almost hated Chrissy for showing up then. He glared at her and the woman chose to retreat, sashaying out the door with an airy wave of her hand.

"See you outside, Rae. Ready when you are." Rae nodded absently, lost in thought for a moment.

Morris Fremont was all but handing her a dream she'd cherished. How, Jase wondered wearily, could he compete with that?

He'd already offered her everything he had, every-thing he was or could ever hope to be. All he could do was ask again, even though he knew it would be futile. "Stay here with me, Rae. Marry me."

Rae cringed as those words dropped into the tense silence, though she'd known they would come.

"You're passing up a much bigger opportunity than the one in that letter," Jase said on a rough, heavy exhalation, "though you won't see it that way."

"But—"

"You came here to capture the craziness Kurt started by advertising for a wife, but you've only caught the surface, Rae."

She raised her chin and looked at him, finally, and he could see that she'd already made up her mind, just as he had known. "I like to think my photographs go a little deeper than that."

"You told me yourself that you can only capture what you feel. So how can your pictures possibly por-tray the loneliness of hundreds of people searching so desperately for love if you didn't see it?"

"That's exactly what I did see, Jase," she said, try-ing to hold on to her patience. She knew she was hurting him, but there was something more in his tone than retaliation, something that made her vaguely uneasy. "It's very sad and touching that love is so hard to find in our society. That's what makes this such a powerful image of our time."

"Yet you can throw away what we have so easily."

"It's not that simple, Jase." She went to him, put her hands on his shoulders. "I can't let Morris down. He's done so much for me. I owe him."

"And that's the only reason you're going."

"For myself, too," she admitted, trying to be gen-tle. His muscles went rock-hard under her hands and she knew she'd hurt him even more. Her heart began to ache, low and dull, throbbing heavily with every beat. She hated what she was doing. Yet she had no other choice.

Most photographers would never be offered such an incredible opportunity. Jase had to understand why she couldn't pass it up—even if he didn't like it. Besides, this didn't necessarily mean their relationship were over.

"I have to go to New York, Jase. I've wanted this so long . . ."

Longer than you've wanted me, and a hell of a lot more, he thought, utterly miserable. "Well, I won't stand in your way."

"I-I'll call you. When I know . . . when I know."

"Sure," Jase said, his smile as unconvincing as her promise.

Rae just stood there, looking at him, her eyes luminous. Jase thought for a heart-stopping moment that she'd change her mind.

But then she turned away, and a few steps took her from the kitchen and out of his life.

He knew it was forever.

Seventeen

Jase's eyes flew open, then closed again, the sound that had awakened him an already forgotten echo. For a disoriented moment, he wondered why his bed was swaying gently from side to side. Then he managed to focus his bleary eyes and found himself looking at the white ceiling of the back porch rather than the one in his bedroom—from a hard, wooden swing two feet too short for his body.

Before he could count all his aches and pains, he remembered what had ripped him from his hard-won sleep because he heard it again. The sound of a car door slamming.

He rolled off the swing, ignoring the twinge of pain in his lower back and rough wood biting into his knees when they slammed into the porch. All he cared about was the vehicle that had made that sound, and when he saw that it wasn't a red convertible, the breath sobbed out of him.

If he were being honest with himself, he'd admit that this was the real reason he'd slept on the porch—because he half expected Rae to come back.

True, it wouldn't have been easy sleeping alone in the bed he'd shared with her, but he'd always been too pragmatic to let things he couldn't change bother him for long.

Until Rae. The sweet memory of Rae was going to bother him for a long time.

Jase climbed to his feet, forcing himself to look at his parents' black explorer. How, he wondered, was he going to explain everything to them? He was still so raw, all he wanted to do was crawl off somewhere and lick his wounds—or at the very least try to forget that his life might as well have ended when Rae walked out of it.

He knew better than to think his mother would let him off so easily. Laura Van Allen's curiosity was legendary, and undoubtedly the real reason his parents had come home two days early.

But when his petite mother wrapped him in a hug, Jase went from thirty-two years old to ten. He wouldn't have traded that moment of unconditional love and comfort for anything, even the questions to come.

"I'll go help Dad with the luggage," he said when she pulled back.

Laura kept her hand on her son's arm. "Your father needs the exercise." She sent her husband a teasing smile as he deposited the first load of suitcases on the porch and headed off for another. "He ate like a horse in Wyoming and didn't do a lick of work."

Before he could come up with another excuse to leave, Laura pulled back and looked into her son's face. "You haven't even shaved yet," she said, running her fingers over his stubbled cheek. "You're usually out somewhere on the farm by this late in the morning, or at least in your office."

"How are Jo and Chase?"

She didn't bat an eye at the change of subject, but a flicker of disappointment crossed her face. "We were hoping for good news, but they've only been married a few months. Anyway, she and Chase are still very much in love. It won't be long before I have a grandbaby." She sighed. "Even though Wyoming is so far away."

Laura looked around the yard. "Where are the girls? It's awfully early for them to be out and about."

He should have known she wouldn't let him off the hook. "You just said it was late."

"For you, Jase, not for two girls from the city."

"Give up, son." Emil hauled the last two suitcases up onto the porch, lifted one foot onto the end of one and rested his forearms on his thigh. "You know your mother won't let it go until you tell her everything."

Jase ran a hand back through his hair, trying not to feel like he was a kid in trouble. His mother had looked at him with the same sort of long-suffering patience he remembered seeing on her face back then, that confess-or-else determination that no one could withstand. Jase had never been able to, even when he wasn't exhausted and heartsick.

"Rae and Chrissy left for Chicago last night."

Laura sighed again, this time with genuine regret. "Oh, no. I had hoped . . . well, never mind. From the time you were a little boy, you wanted to build a house on that hill in the woods. Your father and I know you've been itching to be on your own for a while now, and when Rae arrived . . . Shucks, we thought we'd come home to find you looking at blueprints."

Jase suppressed a curse. His mother couldn't have brought to mind a more painful memory than when he'd shared that hilltop with Rae—unless it was the moment she'd given him the most precious gift of his life.

I love you.

He knew Rae had meant those words. Too bad she hadn't been able to live up to them.

"What happened?" Laura asked gently.

Jase shrugged, trying not to show the agony slicing through him. "It just didn't work out."

Laura snorted softly. "You've brought your share of girls home, Jase. I've never seen you look at anyone the way you looked at Rae. And she was looking right back. You're going to have to give me more of an explanation than that."

Jase opened his mouth to point out that he didn't have to explain anything, but he took a deep breath instead. It wouldn't help him to lash out at his mother, and it would hurt her feelings. Besides, once he told her, maybe she'd leave him alone to . . . He didn't know what he was going to do, except try not to think about Rae any more.

On an outrush of breath, he related what had happened. It felt like he'd lived a lifetime in the last three weeks, but it took only a few minutes to cover the actual events. And when he was through, his mother's only comment was, "I really took first place for that jam? Martha Haggerty must have been beside herself."

"I didn't notice." Only one woman had held his attention that day, and that night . . . That night he'd learned that there was victory in surrender.

"So she chose photography over you," Laura said, returning to the painful subject matter-of-factly. "She's wanted that her whole life and she's only known you three weeks, Jase. And if living on a farm would remind her of a father like that, well . . ." She let her words trail off.

Jase nodded, trying to stifle the anger and frustration he always felt when he thought of Rae's father. It was nothing compared to the way his heart ached when he remembered how easy it had been for her to leave him.

"She had an opportunity she couldn't pass up—and an excuse to run away," Emil said bluntly. "What did you expect her to do?"

"I don't know." Weary beyond comprehension, Jase dropped down on the porch swing. "I was so close to convincing her to take a chance on us. If I'd had more time—"

"You could have had all the time in the world if you'd gone with her."

Emil slipped his arm around his wife, nodding his agreement. "Your mother's right, son."

"I couldn't just take off. Who was going to run this place?"

"This farm has been around almost two hundred years, Jase. I doubt everything would fall apart if you and I were both gone for a couple of days."

"You two are supposed to be on my side," Jase grumbled. "Why are you defending Rae?"

"We're not defending her," Laura said gently. "We just don't understand why you're being so stubborn."

"It's this simple," Emil interjected. "You love the girl and she loves you. The two of you belong together."

Jase clenched his jaw. He'd given one hundred percent of himself to Rae, and then more when she had needed more. Was it too much to want her to make some concessions in return?

Laura folded her arms, glancing over at her husband. "Funny," she said, "I don't remember him being this dumb."

Emil shrugged. "Love's an odd thing, darlin'. It makes the female mind move faster than the speed of light, but I think it kills cells in the male brain."

"That's because there's no blood getting up there."

"There's no need to insult me," Jase grumbled, feeling his face heat. "If Rae had wanted me to come, she'd have asked."

"Maybe she didn't think you'd go," Laura pointed out.

Jase forced himself to think about that. *Really* think about it. He'd never considered living anywhere but Norge Farm. After all, Rae had the portable profession; it would be simple for her to make the farm her home base.

But she had never been able to see the possibility. From the moment she'd arrived, Rae had excluded him from her work. It hadn't only been the fact that she'd kept her real reason for coming to Current a secret. Even after she'd told him about her love of photography, she had gone to great lengths to keep the two facets of her life separate.

And he had let her, Jase realized. He'd sat there last night and let her choose between him and photography, as if there had to be a choice.

Jase dropped his head into his hands. "Okay, so I'm dumb."

With an amused shake of his head, Emil disappeared into the kitchen.

Laura sat down beside her son. "Love isn't something you can think your way through, sweetheart. You can't choose who you fall for, and everyone comes with baggage. Sometimes one person has to make allowances because the other person hasn't unpacked yet. You told me yourself that Rae still loves her father, after everything he's put her through. It's not your feelings she doesn't trust, Jase. It's her own."

Those words, that concept, as simple as it was, absolutely amazed Jase. He stared at his mother as the idea sank into him. *It wasn't him Rae didn't trust. It was herself.*

Somewhere inside himself, he'd known that. His mistake had been in thinking the battle was one she'd have to fight alone.

He passed a hand over his face, weary but knowing the real fight had just begun. He didn't relish the thought of leaving the place he loved, but one way or another he knew he'd see it again. And taking a job in the city for a little while would be a small price to pay for peace of mind. He'd never have that peace until he was with Rae again.

"I didn't go with her, so I guess I'll have to go after her." As soon as the words left his mouth, he knew it was right. It felt like he'd been looking at the world through a funhouse mirror, and everything had just slid back into focus.

Emil clattered out the back door. The scent of fresh coffee from the cup in his hand was almost enough to make Jase fall on his knees and beg. "Did one of the men get that old International tractor running?" he asked, handing the cup to his son.

"Not that I know of." Jase wrapped his hands around the porcelain and took a gulp, ignoring the sharp sting of the boiling-hot liquid. The energy he needed to put his decision into action was at the bottom of that cup. The flavor of fresh-ground coffee exploded onto his tongue and he closed his eyes in sheer pleasure as heat blossomed in his stomach and caffeine jolted into his system.

"I could swear I heard a diesel engine," Emil said. "You know how rough they idle. Now that I'm out here, though, it sounds like it's coming from the road."

Jase looked at his father, slowly realizing that he'd been hearing the rhythmic thrum of an engine for a few minutes, but he'd been too caught up in his own misery to notice.

Even as he tried to tell himself it was nothing, his few functioning brain cells sent him stumbling down the porch steps, then stopped working completely. The cup fell from his nerveless fingers and bounced on the grass, spilling coffee and a rich cloud of steam. He went completely numb except for his heartbeat, thudding slow and heavy, roaring in his ears and throbbing hotly behind his eyes. It wasn't the semi parked across the driveway that stole his wits, though.

It was the sight of Rae walking up the drive.

Eighteen

She looked like a goddess haloed by the dawn, slender and almost inhumanly beautiful.

Jase stared, dumbstruck as she turned and waved toward the truck. An arm poked out the window—a man's arm—and waved back.

Emotion rushed into the void that surprise had left, a hot rush of jealousy that seared his brain, threatening to incinerate the paths of logic and reason.

Rae hadn't seen him yet and he fought for self-control. He knew better than to think she'd take up so casually with any man. He'd had to fight like hell to get her to spend time with him and she claimed to love him.

But he didn't want to let go of the anger yet.

Rae had waltzed out of his life without a backward glance, now she was waltzing back in. To stay, he wondered? And if not, could he stand another day like yesterday? That had been the worst heartache he'd ever lived through, but he had lived through it. Somehow.

Jase wasn't sure it made sense, but going after her would have been a hell of a lot different than having her show up on his doorstep completely out of the blue. He'd wanted to prove something to her and his sacrifice might have accomplished that. Now he was right back where he'd started the day.

No, he corrected himself. There was no way he'd let Rae control the situation this time, even if it meant hardening his heart when all he wanted to do was pull her into his arms.

Jamming his hands into his pockets was better than fisting them, and leaning against the porch railing gave him at least the illusion of nonchalance. But Rae wasn't fooled for a second.

She took one look at his face and stumbled to an abrupt halt. Over her shoulder, Jase saw the semi driver swing down out of the cab of his truck and start toward them. Jase was halfway down the drive before he even realized he was moving.

"You okay?" the truck driver called out.

Rae held Jase's hard brown eyes for a second. "I'm fine, Ronnie," she said. She put her hands to her ice-cold cheeks, rubbing some life back into them before she turned around. "I can't thank you enough for going so far out your way to get me here. I'm sure your wife is worried about you by now."

Ronnie slowed, then stopped. For his sake, Rae hoped he wouldn't act on the warning look he shot Jase, because Jase looked like he wanted to take someone apart.

She caught Ronnie's eyes and smiled. "Go on home."

He glanced behind Jase to where Laura and Emil stood on the porch, apparently deciding she was safe enough. "You've got my number, Rae. Just give me a call if you need anything." He gave Jase with another telling look before he headed for his truck, calling over his shoulder, "I'll see you soon."

Rae didn't draw breath until the semi was nothing

more than a dust cloud heading toward town. Even when she turned around, she couldn't bring herself to meet Jase's eyes. She looked past him, to where his parents stood on the porch. "Welcome home."

"I'd like to say the same to you," Laura replied, "but . . ." Her gaze moved to Jase and then back to Rae. "I'm glad you're here."

Emil grinned and winked, nodding once in encouragement. "I think we could all use some coffee." He retrieved Jase's abandoned cup, then herded his wife toward the kitchen door. Laura went reluctantly, Rae noticed, but she went, sending her a thumbs-up signal on the way.

Tears had been building up for hours, and the warm welcome of Jase's parents was nearly enough to have them spilling over. She closed her eyes and fought back tears, trying to swallow the lump in her throat. She wouldn't have Jase thinking she would cry to gain his sympathy.

She took a deep, calming breath, and let Jase speak first.

"For a woman who doesn't want entanglements, you seem to collect them faster than kite string in a stiff wind."

Rae lifted her chin and squared her shoulders, trying not to crumple into a heap of misery. "Ronnie lives in the next county with his wife and three kids. He was nice enough to give me a ride, and I promised to take their pictures to repay the favor."

"He could just as easily have taken you somewhere no one would ever see you again."

Jealousy—and concern. Rae would have smiled if not for his anger, so much stronger than either of the other emotions. "I . . . needed to get back here, and Chrissy went on to Chicago." She saw the instant flare of something violent enough to be called hatred and rushed to explain. "She had to be at work early this morning, Jase."

"It's Sunday."

Rae smiled slightly. "There are lots of jobs that mean working on Sunday—like farming."

"And photography."

She held his gaze, and Jase thought he saw a challenge in the bright blue depths of her eyes. Every time he tried to channel some of his anger elsewhere, she stepped in front of it. If she wanted to be a target, he'd damn well let her. "Why are you here?"

Rae dropped her eyes. Through the long, sleepless night she'd focused only on getting back to Jase. Now that she'd managed it, how did she answer his deceptively simple question?

"I don't know."

"I thought you'd made up your mind to go to New York."

"I did—I have." Rae closed her eyes, which were burning with fatigue. Her brain was sluggish for the same reason. "Could we sit down?"

Jase saw the way she rubbed at her temples. A closer look showed the exhaustion on her face. She must have traveled all night, and he felt a twinge of guilt for keeping her standing out in the driveway.

He led the way onto the porch, gesturing toward the swing. Sitting next to her would have been a mistake, so he propped one hip up on the porch railing, facing her. Even that was almost too close; he could see every nuance of emotion in her shadowed eyes, and what he saw at the moment was pain. He knew he wouldn't be able to stand it for long without doing something about it. And he couldn't make the first move. Not this time.

"Do you want a cup of coffee?" he asked, staring off toward the kitchen door, more for his own protection than any burning desire for another cup.

Rae pressed her hand to her stomach, murmuring, "No, thanks." She could have used a stiff dose of caffeine to help her get through the next moments, but she doubted she could keep it down.

She'd hurt Jase, destroyed his trust in her—or damaged it badly, at the very least. After turning her back on him last night, she couldn't simply show up, say she'd made a mistake, and expect him to just forget it.

"You still haven't answered my question."

"I'm not sure I can," Rae said softly.

"Either you came back for the clothes you left in my office or something happened between here and Chicago."

The mention of her clothes sidetracked Rae for a second, until she remembered what they had shared in his office. Had it only been yesterday that she had been so eager to show Jase how deeply she loved him? she wondered. It felt like a lifetime ago, and now she wasn't sure he wanted her love anymore.

"Why are you here?"

When she didn't answer, didn't even look up, Jase reached over and nudged her chin up. Sad blue eyes met his. A single teardrop trembled on her bottom lashes before his touch sent it sliding down her soft cheek. Again Rae closed her eyes, trying to dam the flood.

"I left here, convinced it would only be for a week. Two at the most. But then I started telling myself things like, I've got all the photographs I need, and if I had to talk to Kurt it would be just as easy to call him on the phone as to come here in person. The farther away I got, the easier it became to come up with reasons why I wouldn't need to come back."

Rae climbed to her feet, exhausted, but it was hard to admit the truth to Jase, nearly as hard as it had been to face it herself. As much as talking, she needed to walk it out. "I knew if I left here I'd keep coming up with excuses not to come back, Jase. After a few months I'd manage to convince myself that it would never have worked out between us, that suffering the heartache now would be better than waiting for my heart to be broken later."

"And you'd have your brilliant career."

"You were right about that, you know." She smiled, a bittersweet curve of her lips that made him want to fold her into his arms and soothe away her pain.

He didn't move. Rae needed to explain her feelings as much as he needed her to.

"I love photography, but it's not everything to me anymore." She stopped and leaned her shoulder blades against the wall. "It used to be the only thing that made me happy. And then I met you."

Jase straightened then, to go to her.

"What are you saying?"

Rae wiped trembling hands over her wet cheeks, wondering when she'd started to cry. "I'm saying I can't live without you. It doesn't matter where, as long as we're together."

It wasn't easy to be logical with his heart slamming into his ribcage and his arms aching with the need to pull her close. But Jase knew he had to be absolutely sure Rae had considered every possible ramification of her decision. "You've been offered an incredible opportunity, Rae," he said solemnly. "I would never ask you to give it up, any more than I can believe you'd be happy stuck on a farm in the middle of nowhere."

Rae heard her own words thrown back at her and the world seemed to come to a halt. No birds sang, no insects hummed, even the sun in the sky seemed to freeze in place. She took a deep breath, struggling to reconcile her desperate love for Jase with the knowledge that becoming another person to please him would ultimately lead to heartache for them both. "I can't be someone I'm not. My work is a part of me, just like yours is a part of who you are, but we can compromise."

"Are you in it for the long term, Rae? Because I don't think I can go through this again."

"Neither can I. Ever. I love you, Jason Van Allen." He didn't respond. Her heart skipped a beat. "I was thinking I could open a studio in town, do family portraits, maybe some local advertising shots or even state work."

Jase had wanted concessions from her. Well, he couldn't ask for more than to hear her offer to change her entire life for him. He reached for her, crushed her to him, burying his face in her hair and drawing her sweet essence into his lungs. "Funny you should mention compromise."

She pulled back, studying his face through narrowed eyes.

How on earth could he hide the incredible happiness singing through him? "When you showed up I was about to pack a suitcase and head for Chicago." He grinned.

"Do you mean to tell me that you had already decided to come after me?" She shrugged his hands off her shoulders and backed away. "You let me spend all this time groveling for nothing?"

"Once you got going, you were pretty good at it," Jase teased. "I didn't have the heart to interrupt you."

The grin faded from his face, replaced by a look Rae recognized too well. "I don't have my heart at all anymore, Rae." Jase crossed the distance between them, taking her in his arms again. "It's yours. Now and forever. Has been since the moment I turned around and saw you ogling me by the well."

Rae considered objecting to his slanted view of who had been ogling whom the day they'd met, but it felt too good to be held by him again. And when she lifted her face and their mouths met, her only regret was that she couldn't see the way he looked at her, that combination of adoration and desire and soul-deep need that she had taken for granted until she'd walked away from him.

She sank into Jase, realizing with a rush of joy that she'd finally come home.

"It's awfully quiet out there all of a sudden," Emil yelled from the kitchen.

Jase framed her face with his hands, chuckling against her mouth. "I think my parents are eavesdropping."

"I should be embarrassed," Rae said softly, resting her cheek against his chest. "But like you said, Jase, they knew before we did."

He dropped down onto the porch swing, pulling her onto his lap and cradling her head against his shoulder. It felt too good to have her close; he wasn't about to let her get even an inch away. "I'm so damn glad you came back on your own, Rae. I would have come after you, but I was getting tired of fighting."

Rae looked down at her hands.

"Hey." Jase tipped her face back up to his. "Talk to me. There's something still bothering you."

"You said you didn't want me to give up that opportunity in New York. Did you mean it?"

"Do you think I could love you more than my own life and ask you to give up something that means so much to you?" But he knew it would feel like a part of him was gone when she left, and he wouldn't be truly whole until she came back.

"Then . . . would you go with me? Just until I find out if they want me to do the piece."

Jase felt his muscles unlock, one by one, as relief breezed through him. "And then we'll come back here. Either way."

"After this commission, I can get an agent to handle the business end of things. I won't have to travel except when I have an assignment."

"*We* won't have to travel as often," he corrected, burying his face in the hollow of her throat.

"You're sure you won't mind?"

"Now that I know I come first, I think I can handle it if you occasionally get caught up in your work."

"I love you," Rae breathed, her heart so full it felt ready to burst. "I can't even imagine my life without you in it."

"Good, because when we get back from New York we're going to make some plans."

A delighted yell startled them.

"Hooray! I knew it! They're getting married!"

"Laura, at least let the kids think they're surprising us."

"She hasn't said yes yet," Jase shouted in the general direction of the window above their heads.

"Yes," Rae said just as loudly, laughing at the squeal of delight coming from inside the house. "But not right away," she added for Jase's benefit.

"You're not having doubts?"

She clasped her hands behind his neck, looking him right in the eye. "I'm only going to do this once, Jase, and I want to do it right. The church, the white dress, everything."

"How about when I get our new house finished?"

She pulled back. "What are you talking about?"

"You remember when I took you to that clearing in the forest overlooking the lake?"

Rae thought back to that tree-covered hill overlooking the calm lake, the wonderful tranquillity of it, and remembered the magic.

When she didn't answer, Jase brushed his fingertips over her cheek so that she met his eyes.

Rae caught his hand and twined her fingers with his. "It's so beautiful and peaceful there, Jase. I don't think I could bear to see it changed—and anywhere we're together will be wonderful."

Emil poked his head out the back door. "You can convert the row houses, son. Your office is already at one end. Rae can have a darkroom at the other end and that leaves lots of room in between for—"

"We get the picture," Jase said, rolling his eyes

"But I want them to live here," Laura objected, pulling her husband back into the kitchen.

"They need privacy, Laura. And just think how nice it will be to have the house to ourselves again after all these years."

"Hey," Jase yelled. "It's awfully quiet in there all of a sudden."

"I'll handle my love life, son," Emil called back. "You mind your own."

Jase wrapped Rae tight in his arms, loving the way she sighed and melted against him. "That's exactly what I intend to do."

ABOUT THE AUTHOR

Penny McCusker was born and raised in southeastern Michigan, and still lives there with her husband and three children, ages 12, 11, and 6, all of whom are used to sharing her with her computer. THE MARRYING KIND is her third Precious Gem romance, along with HAPPILY EVER AFTER and TWO FOR THE ROAD.